Annie's Guests

Barbara Marriott

International Standard Book Number 0-9723771-0-7
Library of Congress Control Number: 2002094453

Published by Catymatt Productions
Tucson, Arizona 85739, USA
email: Catymatt@aol.com

Book design and production by Kate Horton
Cover photo: Courtesy Oracle Historical Society

Printed in the United States of America

Dedicated to the
Spirits of the Old West
and all those who have the
spirit of the Old West

Table of Contents

Introduction 7

Chapter 1   The Hotel:
             The Mountain View Hotel 11

Chapter 2   The Entrepreneur:
             William Curly Neal 31

Chapter 3   The Hostess:
             Annie Box Neal 49

Chapter 4   The Lover:
             William Bloodgood Trowbridge 67

Chapter 5   The Mother:
             Elizabeth Lambert Wood 91

Chapter 6   The Cowboy:
             George Stone Wilson 123

Chapter 7   The Mine Owner:
             William Frederick Cody 143

Chapter 8   The Prospector:
             Alexander McKay 169

A Final Word 183

References 187

Territory of Arizona Map 190

INTRODUCTION

Tucked into the shoulder of Arizona's Santa Catalina Mountains, in an area splattered by old mines and once working ranches, is a tiny town called Oracle. It's a laid back, off the wall place with a liberal lifestyle. Its independent character started from the day it was named. When the first name submitted to the federal government was turned down, the man who wanted to be postmaster chose the name of a defunct local mine, which was named after a ship that sunk.

Oracle is one of those original small towns that are disappearing from America. Here there is a sense of a community whose roots are deeply planted in Arizona history. Once, long ago, it was the playground and sometime home of a few wealthy people and some very unique individuals. The wealthy came and dressed it up with their money, their values and their lifestyle. The unique gave it its character — its heart.

Some of these individuals moved into the Oracle area for summer living; others as permanent residents. But in the beginning most came as guests of one of the two hotels. The older hotel, the Acadia Ranch, offered four rooms and tents. It was primarily a sanitarium. The newer one, the Mountain View Hotel, had twelve rooms and offered the latest in luxurious accommodations. Although both hotels shared beautiful mountain views, healthy air, and the very pleasant temperatures, they were very different.

The most curious difference between the two hotels was time. Although only a quarter-mile separated the two sites, the Acadia was one-half hour later on the clock. To confuse matters even more, the town of Mammoth, a scant twelve miles away, was a half hour ahead of the Acadia. Two o'clock at the Mountain View was two-thirty at the Acadia and three o'clock in Mammoth at the mines. This may be how Arizona time was invented.

Few old western hotels housed more celebrities than the Mountain View in its prime. This twelve-room territorial inn played host to celebrated writers, national and international politicians, state makers, and colorful characters.

The Mountain View was perfectly located in the village of Oracle whose climate had been internationally acclaimed as beneficial for those suffering from consumption. This had an enormous appeal at a time when 20% of the population suffered from this disease. Actually, what was termed consumption was a catchall phrase for everything from tuberculosis to temporary lung infections.

But the Mountain View was not a sanitarium It was a luxury resort that offered good fresh food, clean mountain air, and all the recreational facilities vacationers today consider mandatory for a top resort. Some people who were ill came for their health. Others came for its luxuries.

The Mountain View Hotel was open from 1895 until the 1950's. Its hey days were from its opening to the 1920s. It was during this time that the wealthy came and so did the pioneer characters. It was not unusual for someone like the future Ambassador to England to be in a room next to a prospector or a ranch hand.

The glorious Mountain View consisted of two buildings connected by a walkway and forming an L. The two-story bedroom building faced the road. Porches ran around all sides on both the second and first floors. The main hotel, now stripped of its porches, is part of the First Baptist Church of Oracle. The second building that housed the kitchen, dining room and ballroom was torn down in the sixties.

As you travel along the main road in Oracle, heading

toward the Control Road to Mount Lemmon, you will pass the Baptist buildings. The older building next to the road is all that is left of the proud and popular Mountain View. Stripped of its porches and its high-flying weathervane, it is a sorrowful structure, downhearted and melancholy. But if you stop for a moment and listen to the wind humming through the grasses, shrilling through the trees, you might hear the faint sound of laughter from guests long gone. For the spirit of the Mountain View has been captured by the giants of granite — the stoic and mystical Santa Catalina Mountains.

THE MOUNTAIN VIEW HOTEL
1894 - 1957

The Mountain View Hotel, Oracle, Arizona - 1909   Oracle Historical Society

CHAPTER 1:
THE HOTEL

Harry Drachman, Georgie and "L.A." Scott waited bleary-eyed in front of Tucson's Coral Stables on Pennington Street. It was 6:30 in the morning July 31, 1895. The sun was well up and the Arizona desert heat was on the rise. From the stable yard, they could hear the noise of a coach being readied for their trip up to the western tip of the Santa Catalina Mountains. Curly Neal, owner of the stage coach line, came out from the office, which faced the dusty street, and told the three impatient men that the coach would be leaving in ten minutes.

Harry grunted something about having heard that before. L.A. merely peered into the near distance thinking of the cool room he had left to come out and stand in the sun. He ran a finger around his collar. Already it was too tight and they hadn't even begun their journey.

Their musings were interrupted by the jangle of tack as the coach and its horses exited the stable yard and halted next to them. George Carpenter bounded off the driver's seat and began tying their luggage on the back of the coach. George had a likable manner, warm and efficient. He had a stiff, sandy mustache which hid his yellow jagged teeth until he smiled. He smiled frequently. The passengers entered the coach and George swung himself onto the driver's seat, cracked the whip, and gave a yell to the horses. The coach lurched forward and the three passengers settled back for their six-hour plus ride to the Mountain View Hotel.

The Mountain View Hotel had only been open five months but already its fame had spread from Phoenix to San Francisco. Annie Neal was known for her excellent meals. The hotel had a reputation for offering the tops in comfort and entertainment. Harry was mostly interested in the healthy air. He suffered from a lung disease and the mountain air was very healing for him. L.A. had some lung problems, but also needed a little relaxation and fun. Georgie Scott was going up to the Mountain View to enjoy a mini-holiday.

The men had minimal conversation. The town roads were dirt but fairly firm. However, it wasn't long before they left Tucson town and the road turned to a dusty trail. The coach skidded all over the trail. Twelve miles out of Tucson, Carpenter brought the coach to a vibrating stop at Marin Point, a stage stop located at the base of the spiky peaks of the Catalinas.

The way station was located behind a ranch owned by a German butcher named Pusch. His ranch was known as the Steam Pump Ranch because of the unique way its well water was pumped.

The three men unfolded muscles aching from the ride and stretched while Carpenter changed horses. The way station stop signaled the worse part of the trip was about to begin. The trail from Marin Point was more uphill than forward.

With fresh horses in the braces, the coach took off, marking its way with a plume of dust. The three were bounced in all directions on the hard seats. It seemed more like trail blazing with the two half-broken horses in the reigns. One of the passengers uncapped a silver flask and politely passed it around. They had a long way to travel.

The coach moved along the Cañada del Oro. The high peaks of the mountains blocked off the east side. On the left, they were bounded by a ridge with undulating rounded hills. Every so often, they would cross a wash, its bed showing no trace of water. Cholla and prickly pear gave way slowly to yucca, and then to small trees. Here and there in the distance some cottonwoods could be seen signaling water. The jagged peaks of the mountains smoothed out, becoming higher, more rounded mountain tops. They passed Castle Rock, Mule Ears, and the shotgun sight. The sun was devil hot and the route was all uphill. They ate dust for most of the trip and used the flask to lubricate their dry throats.

They passed an abandoned ranch with its deteriorating corrals and spied a tent. A woman was busy at the outdoor cookstove but *straightened at the sound of the coach and gave it a big wave and smile. George bellowed a "Hello Mizz Herrera" as the coach bounced past.*

The coach made a quick turn and entered another world. In front of them was a land of green oak and black walnut trees. The grass was so high the slight breeze made waves as it teased the stalks. But that wasn't all. There before them was a magnificent mansion, two stories high and surrounded by an artistic garden. George informed the riders it was the home of Mrs. Steward. He continued that the Stewards were from Joliet, Illinois. Mr. Steward had owned a flour manufacturing business. The Stewards had come to Oracle a few years ago and Mr. Steward had recently died. All this was bellowed out as the coach was moving along at top speed.

Just beyond the stone and wood mansion was a small wooden building in front of a large adobe structure. George identified the wooden building as the general store. The large adobe was the home of the Estill family, the owners of the store.

The passengers were still craning their neck to get a good view of these buildings when the coach came to such a sudden stop. It swayed forward and back for a full minute. Looking around, the passengers saw they were in front of a two-story red brick building completely surrounded by porches top and bottom. Standing on the lower front porch was an Amazon of a woman dressed in white with a colorful bandanna around her head.

She stepped down off the porch. Her soft voice carried into the coach, "Welcome to the Mountain View gentlemen, I'm Annie." The gentlemen were road sore, thirsty and hungry, and ready to enjoy all that the Mountain View had to offer.

In 1895, there wasn't much in southern Arizona territory. Gold and silver fever had produced a few booming mining towns like Jerome, Bisbee and Tombstone. And, there was the major supply town of Tucson, ringed by mountains, and resting in an area like the hollow of cupped hands. The Sonoran Desert surrounded the town, but its saving grace was the Santa Cruz River that ran through the town, supplying it with the most precious of resources in a desert — abundant water.

Tucson was like other territory towns close to the Mexican border. It was desert hot and had a neglected air about it, as if the people who lived there had no future and a past they didn't want to consider. It was undisciplined in the ways of old western towns. The law was defined by whoever wore the official badge, or whoever decided they were the law. Saloons outnumbered churches. Brothels did a thriving business and people went their own way.

Most of the town's visitors were miners who came into town from the gold fields located in the surrounding Santa Catalina, Rincons, Galiuro, and Santa Rita mountains where prospectors were hitting pay dirt. Of them all, the Santa Catalina Mountain Range was the most dominating, its highest apex a rounded mound that reached up over 9,000 feet.

Because of the not too distant ring of mines, Tucson was the closest depot for the train. It was the shipping point for cattle and ore, and a supply center for residents of the surrounding mountain towns. By 1880, it was the destination for prospectors, tourists, and pioneers, all looking to make their mark in the west.

In 1878, William Curly Neal arrived in this territorial town as the driver of an Army supply wagon. The very next year, Curly left the Army, stayed in Tucson and started his climb to fortune. Eventually, he amassed enough hard currency to become one of the wealthiest men in the area with business interests in freighting, ranching and tourism.

Curly's interest were concentrated in the northwest area of

the Santa Catalina Mountains. There, in a hamlet called Oracle, Curly built his most memorable and exciting project — the Mountain View Hotel.

Between 1895 and 1920, Curly's hotel gained a reputation as a luxurious mountain resort that pampered guests from all over the world. By today's standards, William Neal's twelve-bedroom hotel would be considered a small inn. Yet these few rooms sheltered men and women of national and international fame.

Many of its guests helped shape the embryonic State of Arizona. Stratton, Steward, Hitchcock, Ronstadt, Kitt and Drachman signed the register and inscribed themselves in Arizona history. Politicians, show business celebrities, East Coast businessmen, and European royalty came to the Mountain View Hotel, making it one of the most important establishments of its type in its time.

Curly began construction on the hotel in 1894. It took six months to build. Over a thousand adobe bricks went into its two-foot thick walls and each brick was made on the site. Care was taken so that each brick was the same size. A stucco coating was applied over the adobe front and the building was painted red. A talented painter painstakingly drew white lines on the façade to give the appearance of a brick building. The finished product was elegant and unique. But it did not come cheap. It is reported that the construction and furnishing of the hotel cost Neal $90,000.

The Mountain View Hotel was really a complex of several buildings. The largest building with two stories measured 50 feet by 46 feet. It housed the guests' bedrooms. Attached to it by a walkway was a smaller, two-story building that was used for dining and entertainment. The design of the main building was similar to Louisiana French architecture with porches and balconies along four sides. A parapet supporting a sign that proudly proclaimed "THE MOUNTAIN VIEW

HOTEL" topped it. Above it all, racing with the wind, was a weathervane depicting a Hamiltonian trotter. Surrounding the hotel were shacks and bunk buildings for the employees, horse corrals and stables.

The hotel complex was situated on 160 oak-studded acres. The gardens were a mix of wild flora and pampered native plants. Mrs. Neal was an avid gardener and prided herself on her vegetables and flowers, most of which found their way to the hotel tables.

The hotel had twelve rooms, six on each floor, and each room had a shuttered door that opened to the verandah. These accommodations were augmented by wood and canvas tents set up around the main buildings.

The hotel featured the most advanced designs of the day. The craftsmanship was superb. High ceilings were softened by the lacy look of pressed, patterned metal. All the interior woodwork, including wainscoting and fireplace mantels, were of oak and walnut. First floor rooms were outfitted with elegant fireplaces trimmed in black and gold. On the second floor each room had its own free standing stove.

Annie and Curly incorporated every comfort and luxury they could think of into the Mountain View, including a spacious wine cellar under the main building. The bedrooms were furnished with gleaming, brass-knobbed bedsteads and marble-topped tables. Chairs were of solid, squared oak in the Mission style. Annie covered the tile floors with colored art squares that added brightness and made cleaning much easier.

Entering the hotel, you found yourself in a wide hall that extended the full length of the building. At the rear of the hall was a bathroom with running hot and cold water. Annie's office was located in the corner of the back porch. But if you wanted to find Annie, you would first look in the kitchens, then in the music room and then outside by the corral — for Annie was very much involved in the goings-on of the Mountain View and the pleasure of her guests.

At the top of the stairs on the second floor was another large hall with bedrooms located on both sides. The hotel's second indoor bathroom was located at the rear of this hallway. Both the upper and lower hallways served as reception areas and provided a place for relaxing and socializing.

The other two-story building was connected to the main bedroom building by a walkway. This second building measured 21 by 48 feet. The first floor housed the dining room and kitchen. The second floor had a wooden floor that made it an ideal, all-purpose entertainment area. It was in this room that dances and church services were held. Among the furnishings were several pieces for the amusement of the guests, including a player piano and a large billiard table.

Entertainment was a primary concern for Annie so she devised all sorts of interesting events. The Mountain View made available all types of carriages, saddle horses and bicycles for the pleasure of their guests. Picnics, card games, dances, and shooting competitions were part of the many activities Annie offered. At one time, there was a nine-hole golf course, the first in the area. Holes were cut into the ground. The "greens" were made by mixing lubricating oil and sand. This combination gave the course a greenish tinge and a proper country club look.

On the west side of the hotel grounds was a croquet court and an outdoor dance pavilion. On its east side were stables and bunkhouses with a corral constructed of solid mesquite posts and oak cross logs. Because it offered so many recreational facilities, the Mountain View became the social center, not only for guests, but also for residents from Tucson, Florence, Oracle and the surrounding ranch area. Lucile

Kannally of the local KAL Ranch remembered Annie's events as "the most fun she ever had."

Although all sorts of celebrations were held there, none were grander than the hotel's Grand Opening. The hotel was launched in a blaze of glory and much publicity on February 19, 1895. One month prior to the opening the *Arizona Daily Citizen* featured a story on the hotel titled: "A Charming Resort."

People came from all over the state to celebrate the opening of the hotel on Washington's Birthday, and future Governor Sam Hughes covered the all-night event for the *Arizona Star*. The Mountain View grounds were jammed with the guests' wagons, buggies, buckboards and horses. Women had carefully packed their ball gowns for the journey; men brought their best suits.

As soon as the guests freshened up and dressed in their party clothes, the dancing started. The men presented a somber background of black and gray for the brilliantly hued ball gowns of the fashionable ladies. Bedecked in silk, organdy and taffeta daintily accented with lace panels, contrasting ruffles and pert bows, the ladies presented a kaleidoscope of color as they swirled around the Mountain View ballroom. Festivities continued into the morning hours. The music, the dancing, and the free-flowing champagne and wine, provided a night never to be forgotten.

The Mountain View soon became an important resort. The *Los Angeles Herald* described the hotel as "... modern in every particular and finished and furnished so completely and elegantly as to rank as the peer of the best city hotels in all Arizona."

The hamlet of Oracle was also the site of another hotel called the Acadia Ranch, owned by Mr. & Mrs. E. Dodge. It had been established primarily as a sanatorium. The Acadia was a one-story building of local stone, adobe and wood. It featured a front porch and four rooms off a long hallway. Two more rooms were added in 1895. Wooden-sided tents surrounding the main building augmented these accommodations. Cooking was done in an adjacent outdoor kitchen area.

From the beginning there was competition between the hotels but it was more for good fun than for economic reasons. Card game tournaments, shooting matches and horse races kept the competition strong. Annie had a huge Indian "olla" (pot) that was awarded to the winner of the shooting competitions. It was passed back and forth for years and was eventually retired at the Mountain View.

Both hotels were popular. What was the lure of this tiny hamlet located 40 miles from the nearest city? It was not easy to reach, as the trip required travel over rough terrain, through washes and cacti, sometimes in temperatures over 100 degrees. It wasn't a trip undertaken in comfort. The ride took six and half hours in a swaying, bouncing coach that managed to find every rut, every gully, and every rock. Even with a half-hour stop to change horses the passengers arrived body sore and wobbly-legged.

The terrain was not only rugged but held other dangers. Apache renegades and outlaws were active in the area. Wild animals, flash floods and oppressive heat made the trip extremely uncomfortable. The fashions of the day increased the discomfort. Women were bundled in stiff fabrics and multiple petticoats and men in high starch collars and three-piece wool suits. Woman's fashionable leg o'mutton sleeves and huge collars took up space in the tiny coaches, making the interior crowded and stuffy. Despite these hazards, people were willing to make the journey. They came for the clear mountain air and temperatures more tolerable than Tucson.

The first guests at the Mountain View were overflow from the Acadia Ranch. However it wasn't long before the hotel began drawing guests on its own merit.

On July 31, 1895, there were nine guests listed in the Mountain View Hotel register. All the guests, with the exception of Lautaro Roca, were from Tucson. Mr. Roca had come in from Camp Number 2, or "Camp of the Horribles" in Tumacacori, south of Tucson. At a time when all mining camps were known to be wild, unlawful, and rough, it can only be left to the imagination to decide what had earned this mining camp such a distinctive nickname.

L.A. Scott had the honor of being the first name in the new register. Lester was a printer at the Star newspaper office. He listed his home address on Maiden Lane, which was a very busy part of town. Maiden Lane was the location of the red light cribs in the Old Pueblo and formed a wedge with Congress and Meyer Streets.

The Misses Amelia Brown and Anna Taylor, who lived together on N. Stone Avenue, were also at the hotel on July 31st. A notation in the margin of the register shows Amelia Brown and Anna Taylor had arrived on July 23rd.

In the late 1890s, North Stone was one of the more desirable residential communities in Tucson. It was the main road to Camp Grant. Tucson Street Railway chose Stone Avenue for its mule-drawn streetcar route thus making it a very fashionable part of town.

The Misses Brown and Taylor were frequent guests at the Mountain View over the next five years. While there is no record of the ages or occupation, if any, of these two maidens, two things are known about them — they were adults and they were unmarried. The exact nature of their relationship is uncertain. They could have been related, friends, or employer and employee. Amelia, or Millie as she liked to be called, and Anna again visited the hotel in October. This time with a John Brown, who lived at the same address.

John was often a guest at the Mountain View. His occupation of stockman probably made his visits professional, and the Mountain View's luxurious accommodations provided an opportunity to mix business and pleasure.

Harry Drachman was also one of the first guests. Harry was a well-known resident of Tucson. His Drachman Shoe Company, located at 6 W. Congress Street, was in the commercial center of town. His home was on South Main.

Miss Floyda Kennedy did not sign the hotel guest book until August 3rd, although an arrival date of July 16th is inked in the margin. Miss Kennedy's residence was also on S. Stone Avenue several blocks up from Millie Brown and Anna Taylor. Signing in on August 3rd with Floyda were Jessie Hughes and Amanda Laurie Hill. If this was Mrs. J.H. Hughes and Mrs. John Hill, they too lived on Stone Avenue.

It seems as if there was a mass migration from Stone to the cooler climes of the northern Santa Catalina mountains. A luxury hotel, not more than a day's drive, would have enormous appeal to those with the financial ability to pay for the privilege. The residents of Stone apparently could afford such pleasures.

The presence of so many women at the Mountain View without male escorts says much about the freedom and fortitude of territorial woman at this time. While women from the cities of the East were constrained by a vigorous Victorian code of conduct, pioneer woman enjoyed unusual freedom and independence.

The pleasant breezes and lower temperatures of Oracle were an enticement for Tucson residents to make the long trip north in William Neal's stagecoach. They came for varying periods of time. Ed Taylor, a Southern Pacific Railroad brakeman probably came up for a short visit. Ed lived on Herbert Street a little east of Stone Avenue just before Railroad Avenue.

In August of 1895, there were three other Tucson guests registered at the hotel. One was E.W. Bowers who was manager at the L. Zeckendorf & Company furniture store. Mr. Bowers resided on North Church Street, a street of offices and residences.

Tucson had its fair share of lawyers, even in 1895. One of these was Charles Bowman who arrived at the hotel on August 14th. Mr. Bowman practiced law from his office at 19 N. Church, and resided at 287 N. Church Street. Throughout the years, a lot of lawyers stayed at the Mountain View. Mining and ranching brought some; Neal's legal problems brought others.

The last Tucson resident to come to the hotel that summer was A.A. Lysight. Mr. Lysight was a clerk surveyor. He lived on Ott Street in Tucson. Mr. Lysight's visit was probably professional. Oracle and its surrounding towns were growing. Ranch land and mining claims required the services of a surveyor as land changed hands and new claims were filed.

During the next 25 years university professors met sports figures at the Mountain View. Prospectors dined with political and legal types; show business personnel entertained military men. The Mountain View had something for all of them.

The first non-Tucson guest didn't come a great distance. C.C. Ritter listed Mammoth as the place of residence when he or she signed in on August 3rd, 1895. But by the end of the year, guests were arriving from California, Illinois, New York, Colorado and as far away as Toronto, Ontario.

From 1895 to 1920, the Mountain View played host to visitors from 45 states and 13 foreign countries including Russia, China and Australia. The presence of out-of-state guests did not dampen the enthusiasm of the local crowd. They came from the surrounding ranches such as the 3C Ranch or Willow Springs Ranch and from the surrounding towns of Florence, Shultz, Mammoth and San Pedro. The town of Shultz changed its name to Tiger after a visiting mine engineer mentioned he had graduated Princeton University, and their symbol was a tiger. The townsfolk thought that sounded grander than the name of the mine owner.

Although the Mountain View had gained a measure of glory, it also had its share of mystery. This involved the very wealthy Mr. & Mrs. Westray Ladd of Philadelphia. Laura Stroud Ladd was the daughter of one of the founders of the Baldwin Locomotive Works and had been left a fortune. The Ladds had come to Oracle for Westry's poor health. He suffered from lung disease.

Westray Ladd was an architect, and his petite wife, an artist whose flower paintings were on display in many fine galleries. The Ladd's believed in the best. They rode two blood bay saddle horses, which were always sleekly groomed. Their saddles were the finest the Villacruses on Meyer Street produced. Mr. Ladd's elaborate saddlebags held canteens of silver. The Ladds were avid riders searching for roaming cattle with Herbert Bowyer, foreman of the 3N Ranch, making trips to Mammoth and visiting old mines in the area. They kept their riding equipment handy in the Neal's saddleroom in the barn.

One morning, a ranchhand rushed into the dining room and announced that the Ladd's equipment was missing. The young couple was well-liked and no one wanted to give them the bad news. The other guests were forever teasing the Ladds about their favored life, which included real cream each morning while the other guests made do with watered down canned milk. But on this morning, no one was in a joking mood.

Frank Dailey, tall, lank, with a perpetual cigarette dangling from his tight-lipped mouth, rode in from the C.O.D. Ranch to offer his expertise in trailing. Frank had been a double spy during the Civil War. Archie Ramsey, the local deputy sheriff had been out earlier following what proved to be a false lead. He was explosively angry. "To steal a man's saddle means taking away his means of earning a living. Stealing a man's horse is a hanging crime. In my mind so is taking his saddle."

Mountain View guests and locals gathered to discuss the problem. But no one from the Acadia appeared, and that included the owners, Mr. & Mrs. Dodge. Acadia hotel guests felt a sense of superiority and detachment about the incident.

Two young healthseekers, Henry B. Langers and Wilbur Winters, perhaps had the answer but didn't realize it. Their tent was near the tent of a muscular bully who was a bodyguard for Mrs. Monteith and her daughters from Portland. The Monteith party was staying at the Mountain View. The bully was an unlikable character, borrowing horses and saddles that he misused, challenging others in races, then employing unfair tactics such as shouldering his opponent off course, or whipping the nose of the opponents' horse.

Henry and Wilbur had heard rasping sounds and saw a flicker of light in the bodyguard's tent porch the night of the theft. The men crept over to have a look and saw the bully stooping over his open trunk, pushing, cramming, and jamming things into it — and then locking the trunk. The men clearly had a dilemma: should they tell what they saw, as inconclusive as it was? And, there was the reward. The Ladds had put up a $500 reward. Curly Neal added another $100.

Because of their fondness for Mrs. Monteith, and especially her daughters, they decided not to mention what they had observed that night. Meanwhile, the promise of a $600 reward kept locals Frank Dailey, Archie Ramsay, Charlie Brajovich, Joe Castro and others in the saddle following false leads. This included the bodyguard, who made a show of riding out looking for the thief, although he loudly proclaimed the man was probably in Mexico by now.

Since the bully wasn't much help to Mrs. Monteith, she decided she could permanently do without his labor and suggested he seek employment with Bachman herding sheep. The bully and his trunk joined Bachman's sheep herd.

Bachman also hired Henry Langers and his friend Ed. They soon discovered that the bully had certain cooking talents, when he was a mind to do it, and that basically became his job. Meanwhile the ever present well-locked trunk was a source of curiosity for the young herders. Repeated hints and outright requests to see what was in the trunk brought growls, scowls and threats, but little else. One day things came to a head, and it was all over a peach pie.

At the end of a grueling day, the boys gratefully herded their charges into the corrals. On their way to the house, the aroma of peach pie brought them almost to their knees. Sure enough, there on the table, hot out of the oven, stood a juicy golden crust peach pie. They hurried through their mutton stew, dumplings and potato dinner, eagerly anticipating the final coup de grace — peach pie.

When the moment came, the bully placed the oval pie before him, flourishing his butcher knife over it. With theatrical deliberation he cut a piece off of each curved end, leaving three-fourths of it untouched. The two end pieces he slid towards Ed and Henry. Having done the honors, he immediately grabbed a spoon and plunged into the rest of the pie. The boys were incredulous. They couldn't believe the bully was gobbling down most of the pie, leaving them two small pieces. The bully felt this was fair. He picked the fruit, made the crust and baked the pie. It was only right he should get the glutton's share. And he informed them that was the way it was going to be from now on.

It was more than the herders could tolerate. They rose as one from their seats and dove for the pie. Gaining possession they tossed the pie and platter at the bully's hairy chest. The enraged bully exploded out of his seat and reached for the two herders but the table served as a barrier between them and his fists. In the ensuing scuffle, the lean and lanky herders were able to get in several blows. The melee ended abruptly when the herders grabbed a bucket of water and dumped it over the bully, then jammed the bucket on his head. The bucket was a perfect fit — nice and tight — and it succeeded in blinding him. He charged around the room crashing into benches, overturning the stove and finally bursting through the door and disappearing into the dark.

Henry, still enraged by the injustice dealt them over the pie, grabbed an ax and bashed in the lock on the trunk and the heavy straps. They flung back the lid. There they found, jammed in tightly, saddles, bridles, blankets, spurs, riatas, hacamores and saddlebags. The loot from the Ladds.

They couldn't hurt Mrs. Monteith by letting her know the man she had brought with her was a thief. They solved the problem by making small packages of the merchandise and sending them off to friends for Christmas. No one ever saw the bully again. After settling up with Bachman for the damages, the boys headed for Tucson to mail their packages. Very few ever found out the solution to the mystery of the horse gear. One of these was Elizabeth Lambert Wood, who years later, wrote a small local newspaper story about the "Mountain View Mystery."

By the late 1920s, the glory days of the Mountain View

were coming to an end. The building of super luxury hotels in the twenties had a severe impact on the hotel. In Tucson, the El Conquistador provided luxurious accommodations and service. Money was poured into Phoenix by Biltmore and other investors to build resort hotels that pampered and pandered to the rich. From the early twenties until the thirties, the Mountain View had fewer and fewer guests each year. In 1935, Curly and Annie moved off their ranch and back into the hotel.

William Curly Neal died in 1936 — killed in a freak accident in his own front yard. Annie stayed at the hotel until her death in 1950. The Mountain View Hotel went through a series of owners after Annie's death but was vacant from 1941 to 1952. That last year, Frank Brophy, President of the Bank of Douglas; Larry Bell, Manager of the Arizona Natural Gas Service; and ranchers Hank and Jack Freeman purchased the property. It was renovated in the early fifties in the hope of using it as a hotel for the workers who were building the town of San Manuel on the foundations of the town of Tiger. The Magma Mining Company had purchased Tiger — rousting its residents, sometimes with no more notice than a knock on the door and an order to move. Tiger was leveled and in its place rose the "modern" miners' town of San Manuel. This proved to be less than profitable for the Mountain View and it finally succumbed to age and neglect.

In 1957, the Baptist church purchased the Mountain View but because of structural damage had to remove the porches and make other structural changes. Although part of the Mountain View stands today, what is left is only a hint — a ghost of its former self.

WILLIAM CURLY NEAL
1849 - 1936

"Curly" Neal with one of his grandchildren

Oracle Historical Society

CHAPTER 2:
THE ENTREPRENEUR

He lay there a heap of broken bones. Not more than 15 feet away was the instrument of his destruction. Its long black lines glistened from hood to bumper in the September sun.

The car had been one of his few vanities. He always felt a sense of power driving the sleek auto down the roller coaster mountain roads into Tucson. He enjoyed the looks of envy he provoked in town. There weren't many cars around the city that were as elegant as his Peerless.

The somber crowd surrounding him was nothing more than dark shadows wearing halos from the bright sun. From a distance, he could feel the probing and prodding of the doctor's hands. The aches he felt were deep, grabbing him to his soul; a burning, throbbing sensation that made him want to pull within, to shrink away, and to forget. He wanted to talk but words wouldn't come, so he lay there somehow knowing that he would never talk again.

He felt a flutter on his cheek, a soft cupping.

"Curly? It's going to be all right. Dr. Marsh is taking you to Tucson — to the hospital. It's going to be all right."

Ah, his Annie, his wife, "the Cherokee Princess." Her soft voice was a song to him. But no, he knew it wasn't going to be all right, not ever again. He could see the yellow-orange glare of the sun on the inside of his closed lids, but it wasn't warm, it was cold and getting colder.

He felt a stab of icy cold pain creep up from his legs. It was more intense than any Indian arrows or bullets he took in his scouting days. Was that Annie's hand on his forehead? Did she say something, or was that the ancient wind drifting down the mountain slope, parting the high grasses, and stirring the oak leaves?

He remembered that wind. It had caught his attention the day he first saw Oracle. That was 1878 and he was hauling supplies for the Army into Tucson. The Indians were on the warpath, again, so he stayed away from the known routes and took to the rutted mountain trails. About forty miles from Tucson he stopped to water his cattle at a mine site called Camp Oracle.

Resting against the wagon he let his eyes roam the countryside. His first thought was what prime cattle country this place was. As he scanned the horizon his eyes skipped across several near and far mountains. He also thought there might be some good ore there. Good range land, pretty country, maybe someday he would come back to this promising land. His memories faded, he could hear someone speaking: he felt pulling and lifting, then nothing else.

The day Curly Neal stopped at Camp Oracle he began living his dream. Up to that point, his life hadn't been worth much. He was born poor on March 25, 1849 in Tahlequah, a part of the Oklahoma Cherokee Nation. His father was black, his mother a proud Cherokee, tested on the Trail of Tears. He and his mother left the reservation when his father was murdered. Some say he killed his father for beating his mother. Maybe that was why they left. He didn't know. He couldn't remember.

Off the reservation, they lived with two maiden aunts. He was never very happy there, but as long as he was with his mother he survived. Then his mother died and he wanted to die too. He never felt so alone in his life. When he was seven, he ran away and never went back.

He hid in the railroad station, in plain view, shining shoes. He was good at that. He buffed and polished until he could see his black face peering back from the high tops. He polished and smiled and lived on what his efforts produced.

The brakemen started calling him "Curly Bill" because of

the thick, long hair that curled and swirled all over his head. The Indians had called him "Sitting Bear." Curly Bill was probably a better description; he wasn't much for sitting still.

Even then, in the railroad station, he knew there was something waiting for him, something important. That something turned out to be William Cody. He was 19 when he met Bill Cody. Cody was three years older and hadn't yet earned his title of Buffalo Bill. Curly was a bull of a man, full-grown, not very tall but big shouldered, barrel-chested, strong, stubborn and courageous. He never did waste time or words and with Bill Cody around he didn't have to.

"Follow me," said Cody. And Curly did — to territories barely populated, to the wilds of Indian country, to land being broken and crossed by railroad ties and black belching engines. From 1868 to 1872, he scouted with Cody for the U.S. Forces, an occupation with considerable risk. He followed Buffalo Bill and became more than his aide. He became a fellow scout and a friend, forging a relationship that lasted a lifetime. Together, they helped survey uncharted lands, fought the Indians, and killed the wild buffalo for the train barons. Together, they saw new sights and old cultures.

If it hadn't been for Bill Cody, maybe he would still be in some railroad station shining boots and fancy high tops waiting for that something as he watched the trains come and go, his life filled with soot and smoke.

He carried a number of scars from those years and Cody, ever the showman, took great delight in publicly demanding, "Hey Curly, take off your hat and show these people where an Indian bullet plowed your head." People were always impressed at the marks left by the near fatal shot.

He knew if he was to turn his dreams into reality he had to leave the Army. The year after he arrived in Tucson, he severed his connection to the Army and took a job cooking at the Maison d'Arcy restaurant. He also started a business digging cellars. The hours he had to spend on his cooking job kept him from overseeing the cellar digging. Lack of supervision cost him three hundred dollars on his first job.

He needed to find a supervisor he could trust. He found him in Henry Ransom. Henry had recently arrived in Tucson. There weren't many blacks out west. Counting Curly and Henry there were about 150 in the whole Arizona Territory. Because of their small number, the black community in Tucson was a close knit society. Henry accepted the position of supervisor for one dollar fifty a day. That was fifty cents more than the Mexican diggers.

Henry Ransom had a habit of worrying about everything and if there wasn't anything gloomy enough, why Henry just invented something. But there was this one time when Henry's worrying proved to be Neal's good fortune.

The Mexican crews were unhappy. They wanted to be paid at the end of each day. Henry thought it was a good idea to have this money handy. Curly however had a lot of misgivings about having all that cash around; after all it wasn't unusual for a man to lose his money on the streets of Tucson. But Henry kept after him, and rather than hear Henry complaining about how hard it was to keep the Mexican help, Curly gave in.

Curly Neal withdrew his savings from the Hudson Bank that Saturday, May seventh. What a shock for the town when the Hudson Bank declared itself out of business on Monday, May ninth, 1884. If it weren't for Henry's nagging, Curly would have lost his whole bankroll.

The cellar-digging business was proving too unpredictable for Curly. He took his profits and started the Coral Stables, also known as the Opera House Livery Stable on Pennington Street in the middle of Tucson.

Business was good. He was filled with ambitions and good will. From time to time, he would help out a friend or two with a loan. Not all his loans were good ones. When a black friend's cattle ranch folded, he accepted his horses in payment for the loan.

Curly Neal ran his line up to the northern Catalinas, hauling whatever he could. He did pretty well. The Butterfield Stage went near there, but not from Tucson. You had to go to Tombstone to catch it. With the train bringing passengers and supplies into Tucson, a more direct route to the northern mines was needed. For a time, his stage was the only transportation to the tiny northern towns of Shultz, Oracle, Mammoth and the mines that surrounded them.

Talk in town was about a new post office. He never could understand why people didn't listen to talk. He did, and sometimes it paid off. He heard the American Postal Department thought a mail route was needed to the American Flag mining site. More likely, Isaac Loraine and his partner figured it would keep their miners handy if they supplied this service. The partners had struck a main vein and used some of their money to convince people who decided those kinds of things.

Curly went after that mail contract and won it. Since at the time he supplied the only transportation to the northern Catalinas, the decision made sense to him. The year was 1885 and it was going to be a good one for William Curly Neal.

The American Flag's tent city was a sight to behold. There was always activity around the tents. The part wooden frame tents were pitched wherever a level spot could be found. Like most tent cities people added their own touch to make them homier. Curly smiled when he pictured the ingenuity of some of these pioneers. Flags flew outside a few. One or two had pictures painted on the canvas walls. One enterprising family even had an outdoor kitchen in front of their tent. The pipe of the small cook stove was made of haphazardly connected five-pound lard buckets.

Initially Curly's mail route was between Tucson, Oracle and the American Flag mine. The area was growing so fast that it wasn't long before he extended the service to Manleyville, the Southern Belle mine and the Mohawk mine in Mammoth.

There were big changes going on in the northern Catalinas. In 1884, George Fletcher had purchased the Mohawk mine. He hired Captain Johnson to develop the property. Johnson deepened the mine shaft and found the main vein. His next step was to construct a 30 stamp mill on the San Pedro River near the mine. Johnson needed someone who could haul the ore from the mine to the mill, four miles up a hill and 800 feet above the town. The incline was steep and the loads heavy. Strong teams and heavy equipment were needed to move the loads. The newly developed Murphy wagon was the answer. It was designed to haul such heavy loads. With a Murphy wagon and up to 20 horses, Curly could increase his tonnage hauling capabilities.

Curly went to work convincing Johnson to give him the contract and to loan him the money for the equipment. Johnson, like most mine managers, was a clever businessman. He wasn't giving the money without a guarantee. Curly got his money but the contract stated that Curly would pay all the mill's expenses if the ore was not delivered on time. He was as good as his word. He hauled ore on time, and never had to pay the penalty.

With the mail routes and the ore hauling contracts, he was becoming a man of substance. But ambitious men are never satisfied, and he was ambitious. It wasn't long after Curly got the hauling contract that he acquired the contract to provide fuel wood and water to the Mammoth mill and the nearby Schultz mine. Little did he know that it was this contract that would finally crumble his empire, shatter his hopes and deliver a deathblow to his dreams.

As Curly's business grew, the pocket villages of the Santa Catalinas also grew. By 1890, there were over two dozen mines and at least a half-dozen ranches scattered around the mountains and valleys. Mammoth, the next town north of Oracle, was the largest settlement in the Santa Catalina Mountains. It had a population between 600 and 700. It also had a post office and a school. The school had 70 pupils and the town had six saloons.

Curly's life was busy, but on days when he was in Tucson, he would visit with old friends such as the Box family who had arrived in Tucson about the same time as Curly. Hannah Box was a Cherokee who was also a survivor of the Trail of Tears; her husband was of mixed white and black heritage.

Hannah ran a boarding house in Tucson that offered good food and a good bed. Sometimes Curly put up for the night when he was too tired to go back to Oracle, or when he was lonesome. Another reason was the two Box daughters, the child Josie and Annie. Now Annie was far from a child and the two of them became more than friends. She was a beauty with her gleaming chocolate skin and lovely thick hair. Also Annie was not one to be overlooked. She was a proud woman with a regal bearing. Her Papa said she was a Cherokee Princess. She could have been. She looked like a princess; she even acted like one. During her marriage to Curly, this posturing led to some great fights and at six feet tall Annie could hold her own.

Years later, Josie, Annie's little sister, remembered that when Curly visited, he smoked the best cigars and they always smelled so good. "In the winter, he carried a silver flask in the right pocket of his overcoat, and he always had a bag of candy in his left pocket for me." It was a game with both of them knowing how it would end. He would pretend he didn't have any candy, and she would hunt and find it.

When Curly decided it was time to put down roots, he figured Oracle was the place to do it. On April 3, 1890 he paid G.M. Williams one thousand American dollars for some land known as the Anna mine. The property was located just east of Oracle mine on the road to the American Flag mine. Six years later, it was to become the site of the Mountain View Hotel, one of territorial Arizona's premier resorts.

Curly liked to be paid in hard currency. He still remembered the close call he had when his Tucson bank folded. He figured the best place for his money was in land. When the Putnams from Florence put their land up for sale, he bought it. On December 24, 1892, he signed the deed.

The transaction was a strange one. Since some husbands had been known to force their wives to sell out their property, the county official W. L. Van Horn "examined" Lucy Putnam privately and apart from her husband. Now here was Lucy Putnam, ten times smarter than her husband was, and crafty to boot with this county man treating her like she didn't have a brain in her head. Lucy just acted like a sweet innocent, but assured him she did not want to retract the sale, and yes, she signed for the same purposes and considerations as her husband. Having done his good deed, Mr. Van Horn signed the documents. Tough Lucy laughed herself silly while she counted *her* money. If anyone was coerced into signing, it was Mr. Isaac Putnam. The Putnam property was another piece in Curly's land holdings in Oracle and became a substantial part of the 3N Ranch.

Over the years, Hannah Box had acquired property in the Santa Catalina Mountains. The year Curly bought the William's property, Hannah sold the Stonewall and the Merrimach mines to her daughter Annie for the sum of three hundred dollars. He and Annie decided that Annie should sign the deed Mrs. Annie Neal. Two years later, in 1892,

Curly and Annie made it official with a wedding at San Augustin Church in Tucson. He was 43. She was 22.

Annie wasn't Neal's first wife. He was married to Jesús Leon on December 1, 1881. Jesús never understood her husband's need to be somebody, to have something. Annie did. Annie's convent school education had given her a refined outlook on life. She, too, wanted better things than the simple, hard, pioneer life.

Annie could read and write, grow beautiful flowers and play the piano, but her core was tempered steel. Although she had the ways of a lady, she had learned, early in life, how to survive on the frontier. She had spent some of her younger years prospecting with her parents. She could shoot well enough to take on Buffalo Bill, cook up good tasting food from scratch, and beat up most men. Yes, his Annie was a special combination of lady and territorial pioneer. Someone, he instinctively knew, was right for him.

Although Neal's business hauled almost all of the goods and passengers to the Oracle/Mammoth area it was his next contract that brought him the most pleasure. That one was for the hauling of gold bullion from the Mammoth mine to the Consolidated Bank in Tucson.

Just thinking about it stirred his blood. It promised adventure and called for daring and cunning — things missing in his present settled life. He missed the challenges of his scouting life with Buffalo Bill Cody.

Transporting bullion was tempting fate. The mountains, trails, and roads were the highways of bandits. If it wasn't Indians, it was outlaws. They were taking out enough bullion in the local mine for him to make as many as two trips a month and he was determined to be clever.

He figured you didn't have to rob a stage to know how to rob a stage. His first precaution was to not stick to a schedule.

He didn't use the same carrier. Sometimes it was his stage, other times a buckboard or a wagon — sometimes he traveled on horseback. No one ever knew when or how that bullion was going to travel. Still, he was a cautious man. He built clever hiding places into the various vehicles he used. Once he showed George Wilson, a young hotel guest, the hole he had carved out in the tongue of a wagon. He used several routes, including a long Oracle-Redington-Benson-Tucson route. That route formed almost three-quarters of a circle. He usually traveled alone but on occasion would take Annie as guard. She sat next to him atop the wagon, cuddling an imposing rifle.

Maybe it was these devious methods, maybe it was luck, or maybe it was Annie's rifle, but Curly never lost a bullion shipment to bandits. However, the one force he couldn't outwit was Mother Nature.

On that memorable day it was clear and cloudless. The sky was a deep Arizona blue bringing welcome weather after the mountain storms of the past week. As Curly approached Box Canyon he picked up the faint sound. It reached his ears as a low hum. He recognized it pretty quick and knew he had only minutes to react. He looked around for a way up the ridge but all he saw were sheer cliffs. Time was running out. With more strength than even he knew he possessed, he threw himself from the wagon seat, grabbed what handholds he could and scrambled to the top of the ridge. He just cleared the trail when the wall of water crashed into the wagon and team. His six mules were tossed about like straw figures. The water carried them down and under. His wagon was crushed against one side then the other until nothing but splinters remained.

It was a close call and Curly felt mighty lucky to have escaped with his life. The cuts and bruises of his climb were nothing compared to being in that wall of water.

Curly searched for months for the two ingots he was carrying, but never found them. For a long time that canyon was the focal point of every hopeful looking for an easy strike. Curly's reputation for honesty was so strong that no one ever believed he had taken the bullion. However, no one ever found the gold, which means that somewhere in Box Canyon are two ingots resting in mud.

Meanwhile, he decided to put his Oracle land to good use. He set up a ranch and named it the 3N. Curly was a scout, and frontiersman, but he was not a rancher. He went looking for one and found Herbert Bowyer. Herbert was an Englishman with considerable cattle experience. In January, 1892, Curly hired Herbert Bowyer as foreman. Bowyer did well and by the early nineteen hundreds the 3N Ranch supported ten thousand head of cattle plus a herd of goats and a drove of hogs. He rewarded Bowyer by making him a partner in the 3N.

In 1894, he and Annie lost a friend. Annie's mother had suffered for years from dropsy; she never saw the end of that year. Annie was totally distraught. She lost weight and interest in everything and everybody. Curly tried many ways to cheer her up, but nothing worked. He decided she needed a project. Something different, something to capture her interest, keep her busy.

As a true territorial entrepreneur, he was always looking for a new venture to make money. He had noticed how profitable the Acadia Ranch in Oracle was. He thought that someday he might try the hotel business. But he was not a people man. He'd rather do than talk. Now, Annie, she was full of good cheer and good deeds. Loved to spend her time with people, loved to make them happy. Why people couldn't make themselves happy, he didn't know.

Thinking about it, he realized that a hotel was the project for Annie. And, he knew he had the perfect site. He had never given too much thought to his Oracle property — a pretty land covered with oaks and lush grasses. From every angle there was a view of near and distance mountains coloring the horizon in grays, purples and browns. It was the ideal spot for a resort hotel.

He told Annie about it that night. It was just the magic needed to bring her about. He had his feisty wife back. They started building in 1894 and he didn't have a peaceful moment the whole year. Annie saw to everything. She badgered the workers; she nagged him about money; she argued with furniture makers. In the end he spent over $90,000. The hotel opened in February, 1895 with an extravagant, buster of a Grand Opening. People came from all over the state and as far away as California to drink booze and dance all night.

Annie hadn't minded that the Mountain View's first guests were the overflow from the Acadia Ranch. That didn't last long. With Annie in charge, the Mountain View came into its own. Within five years, it became an internationally-known resort. The rooms were filled with important people such as Buffalo Bill Cody, Whitelaw Reed (Ambassador to the Court of St. James), Frank Hitchcock (Post Master General of the United States), Harold Bell Wright (author), and even some royalty including a Russian Prince and two Italian Countesses.

Annie was in her element. Curly tried to avoid the hotel as much as possible. All those fancy folks were a little too rich for his taste, except of course for Bill Cody and some of the mining men. Under Annie's guidance and supervision the hotel blossomed and became known as one of the finest resorts in the southwest.

However, at the turn of the century, the west began changing. A new type of pioneer was arriving. Easterners were coming to Oracle and spending more time. About 30 to

40 year-round residents lived in Oracle with the number escalating to over 300 in the summer. And, all those easterners brought their eastern ways and eastern values.

Other factors were impacting on the wild western frontier life. The Federal Government passed new laws that restricted free grazing on government owned land. The 3N had over 10,000 head and needed the grazing land. Curly thought he could get the land by increasing his own holdings. He applied for homesteading rights. His application was denied. The government told him there were no more rights being granted, then turned around and gave Mr. Herrera from the Oracle area, homestead rights.

Now, it was not in Curly's makeup to take that. He appealed the decision. It took over two years for the case to be settled, and in the end he lost. He carried the newspaper report around with him for years. He would take it out of his back pocket, carefully unfold the yellow sheet and read what the *Arizona Daily Star* had reported on February 29, 1908.

"Commissioner General Gallinger of the General Land Office, Washington D.C. has made a decision in the Oracle town site case in which he upholds the contention of the residents of the city, their clients, and thus takes away from the Negro Neale his claim to have homesteaded the land on which the town is situated." The article goes on to report that he could not be granted homestead rights as the town was incorporated. There is no record of that so called incorporation.

Prior to this, Curly never thought of himself as a Negro. He never thought of Annie having mixed blood. He never gave a passing notion to white men marrying black women, or Mexican women marrying Anglo men. People were just people, good or bad. However, when East Coast residents came — color and customs became important.

It was sad times for a man of color. It got so bad in Tucson, that in 1912, the school board didn't fund a school for black students. A new group called the Ku Klux Klan was parading openly. Things just got worse. In 1931, administrators in Tucson fired all their black city workers and replaced them with white workers.

Gradually, Curly realized what was happening. In Oracle, he and Annie were always invited to the parties and socials. Annie especially seem to be a favorite, and townsfolk were always talking about what a kind woman she was. But then the invitations stopped. The only time Annie was invited anywhere was if they were collecting money or selling something. Annie went. She was too kind not to, and she always gave. But when it came to the teas, and parties, and dances there were never any invitations. He didn't care, but he read the hurt in Annie's eyes.

Just when he thought things couldn't be any worse, old Dodge from the Acadia accused him of cutting too many trees down around Oracle. Dodge and a few others complained to the government. Curly had been hauling wood from unsurveyed public domain land, which was allowed. These loads were mostly dead and rotting wood.

Now maybe, he had cut down a few more than most. After all, Curly had to fulfill his contract for supplying fuel wood to the Mammoth mill and the Schultz mine. But, he knew he wasn't the only woodcutter. However, his stubbornness contributed to what happened next. He should have paid the fine. But no, he knew what the townsfolk were up to, and he just refused to give in. After all, he was William Curly Neal, owner of the Mountain View Hotel. Most of the townsfolk had been guests at his hotel.

So he sued. He chose to fight with Tucson, Phoenix and finally Washington lawyers. None of them helped. He lost the case. By that time, it didn't matter much as the demand for wood burning fuel was almost non-existent. The mills were now using petroleum for their primary fuel.

What money the homestead case didn't take, the wood case did. He was close to financial ruin. Of course, he still had the Mountain View.

World War I was good for the Mountain View. Its rooms were filled with Americans with war money and Europeans escaping the ravages of their homeland. Hoping to create a monopoly on inn accommodations in the Santa Catalina Mountains, he purchased the Acadia Ranch Hotel in 1914. He and Annie ran the Acadia for nine years as a sanatorium.

Things started to go downhill around 1923. He sold the Acadia Ranch for its mortgage to William Trowbridge. Trowbridge had been one of the earliest guests of the Mountain View. His first visit was in 1898 and he'd show up every two or three years after that. That year, Trowbridge also bought the Triangle L Ranch in Oracle for his permanent home.

Curly kept hoping during those lean years that he would get a new mail contract or some new mining contracts. The Young brothers, millionaires from Iowa, had obtained an option on the Mammoth-Collins claim group. Curly figured he would be able to pick up a hauling contract from the new mine operators. Then the brothers negotiated an agreement with Pinal County for the repair of the Oracle-Mammoth road to the Pima County line. By the end of the year, the Youngs were using two three-and-a half ton motortrucks for hauling fuel, machinery, pipes and other supplies from Tucson to the mines. A ton hauled by truck cost $12, hauling by freight team jumped the cost to $15 a ton. A team could make only one round-trip a week while a truck made a round trip in two days, sometimes one. These innovations effectively put him out of the competition for any major mine work including hauling contracts.

If that wasn't enough, the Mountain View was receiving fewer and fewer guests. European money was tight. New advances in medicine kept consumptive sufferers closer to home, and the local mines were closing. Annie and Curly had no choice but to move into the Mountain View Hotel.

Living in the hotel had one big benefit. Curly was just across the street from his grandchildren. He and Annie had adopted Josie when their mother had died. The Neals thought of her as their daughter and not Annie's little sister. Josie had been married to Shad Bowyer, brother of Neal's ranch foreman and partner. Since her divorce, she and her children were living across the street from the Mountain View in the Gable house.

Curly and his grandson Ed liked to work on his car together. The car could be stubborn and, on this day, he had trouble with the starting crank. He looked around for the right size wrench and not finding it, walked over to his nearest neighbor to borrow some tools. When he came back he yanked back the hood and started probing. His grandson was in the front car seat awaiting instructions from Curly. Curly straightened and turned, but not in time, the car kicked into action. Years later, an old timer remembered that "Mr. Neal was hit right in the back by that car."

It was 1936 and William Curly Neal was 87. Dr. Cody Marsh rushed Curly to Saint Mary's Hospital in Tucson, but it was too late for the old entrepreneur; his internal injuries were too severe. Curly Neal never made it back to his beloved Oracle. He died in the Tucson hospital.

Annie carried on as best she could, but finances were tight and on July 16, 1937, Annie sold the 3N land including 100 head of cattle and all the equipment on the land to Herbert Bowyer for the sum of ten dollars.

ANNIE MAGDALENE NEAL
1870 - 1950

Annie Neal with a young Oracle resident

Oracle Historical Society

CHAPTER 3:
THE HOSTESS

The robust music swirled around Annie like campfire smoke. It filled the hotel's hallways, swept out to the brilliant night and rose to greet the Catalina Mountains. It was a night made for music, her night, the Grand Opening of her hotel.

The music ended and the guests surged towards the wine and champagne rooms. Their chatter replaced the music but Annie didn't hear their words for she was filled with the orchestra's melody. Music was very much a part of her; it was her soul and it had been her survival. It gave her courage when she was faced with numbing fear, made her happy when she was sad, and produced pleasant memories.

She wandered out the front door and headed for the corral. She hadn't had much time to herself these past six months. The hotel had taken longer to construct than Curly had planned. But then, she had insisted everything be perfect from the hand-made adobe bricks to the solid square furniture. Now it was done and she was taking this moment away from the party for herself.

*She leaned her back against the corral fence and admired the brick red buildings that formed the L of the hotel. Just then, the moon popped out of a cloud. The orchestra took that precise moment to begin a sentimental rendition of **Silver Threads Among the Gold**. Her eyes made a sweep over the buildings, gardens and the mountains. Tears welled up as she remembered her Momma would never see this glorious hotel.*

Annie Magdalene Neal was an impressive figure. She was over six feet of pure woman, straight as a saguaro, with milk chocolate skin and deep brown eyes that could nail you to the spot. Her spotless, white shirtwaist with its nipped-in waist emphasized her height, and her black hair was pulled into a top bun covered with a neat scarf. You just couldn't overlook Annie, especially if she was bearing down on you.

If Annie in full flight didn't get your attention, her voice and manner did. A woman that big and imposing had to have a voice to match. But Annie's soft words, gentle voice and refined manner were startling because they were unexpected.

Annie was a collection of contradictions. Her physical beauty was the result of an eclectic heritage. Annie's father, Wiley Box, was the son of a white English physician and a black woman from New Orleans. Her mother claimed a German father and a Cherokee Princess mother.

Annie came from tough stock. Her mother, Hannah, had survived the Trail of Tears, that infamous trek from North Carolina, and at age 16 gave birth to Annie on an Oklahoma reservation. Annie made her appearance on a bleak and cold January 8 in 1870.

Annie's genteel character, however, was the product of the Catholic Sisters at St. Joseph's Academy. It was at the academy, where Annie learned the niceties of life. Not everything there was easy for Annie. Sister Eu Frazeer tried her best to teach Annie French, without any great success. However, Annie's main interests were not in books but in the kitchen and the music room. She followed Sister Cabello around the kitchen, helping when she could, mostly getting in the way, but learning the whole time. The fact that the Mountain View Hotel was known for its food attested to how well Annie learned her cooking tasks. In the music room, Sister Clare taught Annie to play the piano and in the process instilled in her a lifetime love of music. Annie had a natural musical talent. She published her first composition, *Oklahoma March*, with the help of Mrs. Mansfelt. Mr. Mansfelt owned the Tucson Pioneer News Depot on Congress and Warner.

The piece was inspired by Annie's journey to Tucson when she was nine. Wiley Box had yellow fever and it was decided to leave the reservation and the bitter winters of Oklahoma and head toward a healthier desert climate.

In 1879, the Box family joined their wagon to a small wagon train heading for Arizona Territory. Travel in the west was always a dangerous activity and renegade Indians and outlaws made it even more so. But the biggest threats were the desert and the wilderness. That experience was burned in Annie's memory forever. She was exhausted and frightened the whole trip, but what she remembered most was her great thirst. Water is a rare commodity in the desert and Annie never got enough of it.

The weather provided more misery for the child. Most nights Annie shivered so much from the cold she couldn't sleep. It was hard to get warm, as campfires were not allowed "lest the Indians spied them." The journey was far from comfortable. The terrain was nothing but mountains and valleys. The wagon didn't have much in the way of springs and Annie's bottom was continually being slapped up and down on the seat, or airborn. The wagons were extremely awkward and could only be held upright on steep hills by chains and ropes.

Tucson was not an impressive sight in 1879. The town was so primitive it was accused of having more dogs than people. Its houses were one-story affairs with flat roofs, which made them look lower and squatter. Some visitors had unkind impressions of this territorial town. Dr. Adolphus Henry Noon of Chicago visited the community in 1879 and noted that the adobe houses were extremely weathered, the windows small and the doors rough and unpainted. In the plaza, the squared Catholic Church, called St. Augustin, had a tumbled down appearance. The streets were narrow and there were no sidewalks, city lighting or waterworks.

The streets were dirt. Swirling dust continually landed in your eyes, mouth, and hair except during monsoon when the dirt turned to sucking mud. The trees and bushes were mostly prickly cacti, creosotes, mesquites and acacias. However, running along side the town was the Santa Cruz, a river that brought enough water for the shady cottonwoods and the residents.

The arrival of the Box family in Pima County raised the black population considerably. The total number of blacks in the County in 1879 was 57. The arrival of the Boxes in Tucson also coincided with the arrival of a black man called William Curly Neal.

When Annie got to Tucson, she was sick of traveling. Papa must have known how she felt. He decided to put her in St. Joseph's Academy, "to get an education" as he put it. As soon as Annie was settled in the school, her parents went prospecting leaving Annie to the mercies of the Sisters at the academy. Mamma and Papa were vagabonds and had been as long as Annie could remember. Although her father professed to be a ship's carpenter, he spent most of his time prospecting and gambling. He did try stagecoach driving and even manual labor at various times, but mostly he found the gambling profession more to his liking. Hannah Box contributed her share to the family income in any way she could. At one time, she made quite a bit of money gathering and selling unusual colored rocks. Eventually she operated a Tucson boarding house.

At fourteen, Annie became ill and had to leave the academy. For a while, she traveled with her parents, prospecting in the local mountains. The next year Annie's life underwent a considerable change. She had grown into a striking woman who was described as both beautiful and kind. Being somewhat of a flirt, it wasn't surprising that Annie attracted suitors when she attended the dances at the

Tucson's Carillo Gardens and Ft. Lowell. At one of these dances, she met a soldier named James Lewis. They were married soon after and Annie and James went off to his next posting in Yuma.

Meanwhile, Hannah and Wiley did not fare as well. George Hand, a handyman for the town of Tucson, documented the events in his diary. On June 15, 1885, Hand's diary notes the local newspaper published this report: "Wiley Box and wife were put in jail on complaint of John Bryson who claims that they robbed him of $1,000." Hand continued to follow the trial noting that on June 25 there was "nothing new but the Box family and witnesses failed to get bonds and are still in jail." On July 7, Hand reported that bail was set for the Box family at $15,000 each. He was a little off in his information. The bail was actually set at $1,500.

The case took a malevolent turn when charges of poisoning were issued. Hand noted in his diary on October 2, 1885 that "one witness in the Box case attempt to poison John Bryson, being absent, the court adjourned till tomorrow, 10 a.m. The defending witness was Cline, `a Negro' who said he was hired to give Bryson poison. Cline was in jail a long time and was finally let out on bail and skipped the country. Everyone from the judge down know all about it, but the judge ordered the sheriff to call Mr. Cline, which he did, but Cline was too far away to hear his call."

It seems unsavory characters were on both sides of the law. Hand reported that on November 5, 1885 "the jury in the Box case went to breakfast at the Elite. They are a filthy set having nothing to amuse themselves with, they very deliberately pulled all the dirt and old papers from the stove and threw them on the floor last night and they will lie there until the jury leaves the room." Finally on November 7, the trial reached a conclusion. Hand wrote "Mrs. Box on the stand all afternoon ... (the jury) brought in a verdict of not guilty."

Meanwhile, during this long process, Wiley was in touch with James Lewis, Annie's husband. On September 2, 1885, he wrote the following letter:

"Dear Soninlaw (sic) I received your king and welcome letter and it afforded me great pleasure to hear from you. My trial comes of about the 12 or 13 of (this month) being put of on account of my attorney being absent. I will write to you the last of the week and explain matters better. Do not send ticket until my trial is over."

Wiley went on to caution Lewis to . . .

"be very particular how you write as I have to have my friends on the outside to write for me. I close - send much love to all. I remain Your true Fatherinlaw, Wiley Box."

It is presumed that love to all meant love to Annie as well.

Apparently, the jury found Wiley as well as his wife to be innocent. Wiley wrote another letter in early November:

"Dear son. I write you these few lines to let you know I'm free. The jury brought in a verdict of not guilty Saturday night. I leave for the line of Mexico as I am flat broke without a cent. Address your letter to Tucson and I will have them forwarded. With love to all. I remain your father, Wiley Box."

Eventually the Boxes returned to Tucson bringing with them a new daughter, Josephine. Hannah opened a boarding house and Wiley went off prospecting, gambling and finding other ways to make money. After the Boxes returned from Mexico, Curly Neal became a frequent visitor to their home and often stayed overnight. While Hannah and Wiley were in Mexico, Annie's marriage to Lewis ended. Annie, ever the ebullient optimist, soon married again, this time to William Easton on April 5, 1887. However, that marriage was also doomed to failure.

It wasn't until January 4, 1892 that Annie ventured into her third, and what was to be her last, marriage. It was on San Juan Day amid the celebration activities of horseraces and dancing that Annie married the family friend William Curly Neal. The ceremony took place at San Augustin Cathedral in Tucson and they took up residence in the Oracle area in a little house Curly built.

It was not Neal's first marriage. County records show he had married Jesús Leon on December 1, 1881. There is no record of what happened to that marriage although there is a record of one Jesús Leon being buried in the Leon family cemetery in the 1900s.

It may have taken her awhile but Annie finally wound up with the right fella. Bull-headed and stubborn as he was, Annie realized that Curly supplied the stability her flighty nature needed while she supplied the elegance and graciousness that he lacked.

That's not to say the marriage proceeded without problems. At times, the hills of Oracle rang with the Neals' arguments. Although Annie was soft spoken by nature that didn't keep her from having some real shouting matches with Curly Neal, after which she would take herself off to the Acadia Ranch Hotel, leaving Curly to stew and handle the Mountain View on his own.

On April 9, 1894, Annie's world shattered. Hannah Box had died at ten p.m. in her home on Pennington Street. The next day the *Arizona Daily Star* reported that: "Mrs. Hannah Box passed away Sunday night after having been a sufferer for nearly two years of dropsy."

Annie was devastated. She lost interest in everything including her music. A worried Curly tried to console Annie but nothing would shake her from her depression. Finally Curly decided that Annie needed a major project to occupy her time, one that would call upon her many talents.

For years he had thoughts about a grand hotel in Oracle. The Acadia Ranch, the only hotel there, was more a sanitarium. A hotel would take up Annie's time and make use of her multitude of talents.

Curly could more than afford the luxury of building Annie a hotel. He was considered very well off by frontier standards. He owned property in Tucson and Oracle, had a lucrative mail route, a thriving stagecoach business, a bullion delivery contract and the Mammoth stamp mill fuel contract.

Thus, it was that at forty-six, past his prime for the times, Curly began construction of the Mountain View Hotel. So much attention was given to making this a fine hotel that it took six months to build and was formally opened on Washington's Birthday in February, 1895. It was a night Annie would remember for a lifetime.

The Grand Opening of the hotel was the first of many successes for Annie. Folks attributed the popularity of the hotel to Annie Neal. Her graciousness was noted in a 1896 article in the Los Angeles *California Herald* which declared: "Mrs. A. William Neal, one of the most charming, genial and appreciative of landladies, who understands how to perform the difficult art of providing the best accommodations including a bill of fare, so as to make all feel pleased, at home and perfectly at ease."

That same year on August 6, the *Tucson Citizen* said this about Annie and her hotel: "Mrs. Neal is the queen of hostesses and that to find such a hotel and such service so far away from the railroad is like a pleasant dream."

Ironically, it was Hannah Box who not only supplied the motivation for building the hotel, but also helped Curly get into the cattle business. The Boxes had acquired mining claims in the northwest foothills of the Santa Catalina

Mountains. Some came from Hannah's boarding house guests who could pay their bill in no other way. Other claims came from Wiley Box's gambling and prospecting activities. As early as 1881 and 1882 Pinal County Court House records have land transactions in the names of Wiley Box and Hannah Box, most of these are mining claims.

A twice-stung Annie was undoubtedly reluctant to rush into marriage for the third time. But Hannah knew she didn't have long to live and using the lure of land, the worried mother attempted to secure her daughter's future. She knew Curly Neal to be a good man, and one who could provide quite well for his wife. Hannah got her wish just before she died.

In addition to the mine claims, Neal acquired several other claims from his mother-in-law and it was these claims that became the 3N Ranch. Neal hired Herbert Bowyer as foreman of the ranch. The division of labor was clear-cut. Curly was the boss of all, Bowyer ran the ranch and Annie ran the Mountain View.

Besides being a sterling hostess, Annie had other talents that Curly appreciated. Like her mother Hannah, Annie was a mid-wife and had the Catholic Church's authorization to baptize babies. Serving in these capacities, she became godmother to most of the children born around Oracle in the early days.

The Academy education may have taught Annie fine social manners, but it did little to bridle her wild spirit. She could handle a coach team as well as any man. The wilder the team, the better for Annie. She was also a crack shot and in later years enjoyed challenging members of Bill Cody's Wild West Show when they came to visit the Mountain View.

Because of her sharp shooting ability, Annie sometimes rode shotgun for Curly on his bullion runs. In those days, it was hard to tell the good guys from the bad but Annie was never shy about using her rifle. So it is strange that on one trip, for some inexplicable reason, she held her fire when she spied an Apache galloping over the ridge. In that split second of hesitation an Army patrol crested the ridge. Seeing Annie posed for action atop the wagon they hailed the duo and explained the Indian was a scout and not a renegade. A sheepish Annie lowered her gun.

With the Mountain View, Annie had found her place in life. She had a venue for her sense of the elegant which she displayed with her hosting skills. Just as the Mountain View was good for Annie, she was good for the hotel. The Mountain View became know as a resort that offered excellent meals, comfort combined with a pleasing ambiance, and a choice of exciting, fun activities. These activities included riding, golf, croquet, dances, picnics, cards, hunting and shooting competitions.

Annie and Curly loudly proclaimed the assets of their resort in California and Arizona papers with advertisements such as this one that appeared in the *Tucson Citizen* on October 6, 1898: "Those desiring to escape the heat can do well to visit the only resort in the territory, the Mountain View Hotel, Oracle where the comforts of home can be enjoyed with the cool breezes day and night. Rates are $10 and $12.50 per week."

However the Mountain View was not to everyone's liking. Eugene M. Sawyer, a mining engineer in the employ of the Copper Queen Mining Company, had an unpleasant experience with Curly Neal. Neal had promised him an early departure from Tucson, but a delay caused Eugene and Curly to get caught in a monsoon shower, which closed off their route for over an hour. An aggravated Eugene arrived at the Mountain View Hotel after six p.m. He refused to stay at the hotel or leave his horse there, so off he went traveling about

25 miles in the pitch dark. He arrived at his destination after midnight. That happened in early September, 1910. It seems Eugene carried a grudge a long time. In 1912, he was back in Oracle again where he spent the night with the Trowbridges. "They are nice people," he wrote home, "and it is nice to have a place to go down there. I don't like Neal's Mountain View Hotel."

Not many shared Eugene Sawyer's view. The Neals were successful and highly respected members of the Oracle community. While Curly was not the most social of men, he was considered honest, dependable and hard working. Often, the local ranchers would seek his opinion on matters. He had strong values and beliefs on fairness and held to them. He once sued a man for $200, charging that he killed one of his goats.

Annie, on the other hand, was outgoing and had a kind and happy nature that won her uncountable friends. She was a generous woman who particularly loved children though she never had any of her own. Annie took care to meet her guests' needs in a gracious and complete manner. She once hired teachers from the East and maintained a private school for the children of the families staying at the hotel.

Since there was no church in Oracle in the early days, Annie arranged for a Catholic priest and sisters to come up from Tucson once a month. Services were held in the recreation/music room on the second floor.

When Hannah Box died, Annie insisted she and Curly adopt her six-year-old sister, changing her name to Neal. When Josie married Shad Bowyer, the brother of Neal's ranch manager in 1911, Annie invited the whole town of Oracle and most of the population around Santa Catalina to the wedding and reception at the Mountain View. It was an exciting and interesting day, never forgotten by some. George S. Wilson, one of the guests, remembered the event well for it was there that he met his future wife. It was also the site of one of his more amusing fights.

Annie's kindness and generosity extended beyond her hotel guests and her family. She left a legacy in the town of Oracle and locals still talk about how "Nobody went hungry when they stopped at Annie's; she'd feed anybody that came around."

When the father of one of the Oracle children died, Annie stepped in and brought up the eight-year-old while his mother worked to support the family. She helped many families and descendants of those families still remember Annie's kind ways. One woman credits Annie for many generous deeds: "she helped my mother in tough times and taught me how to cook, clean and what I know. She was the one that taught me everything I know. When I got married, Mrs. Neal gave us one of the largest weddings there ever was here in Oracle. It was held at the hotel. We had the dance at the Oaks (a local bar and nightclub). They served dinner all day long and after we got married, we lived there with her for six months, and from there we moved to another place, they use to have some cabins back there."

During World War I, the Mountain View was filled with military personnel on leave, government officials, and foreign guests who were escaping the ravages of their homelands. Feeling very much a part of that war, Annie gave a series of Victory Dances to benefit the Knights of Columbus War Fund. She and Curly gave generously to Bond Drives. In one drive, Curly contributed $1,000 and Annie gave $500 more in her own name.

In 1913, another family tragedy struck. Annie's father, Wiley Box, died in unusual circumstances. After Hannah's death, Wiley had been staying in the quarters of an old-club in Tucson that catered to black men on Court Street, between Pennington and Myers. He was a hard drinking man all his life and in his old age, physically unable to do the prospecting that had kept him active when he was younger. He turned more and more to drink. It eventually contributed to the circumstances that led to his death.

After several days of hard partying, Wiley fell asleep in a drunken stupor. His friends, still in a party mood, decided to play a practical joke on him. The practical joke turned into a deadly game. They painted his feet red, wrapped his legs in gunnysacks, saturated them with wood alcohol and set them on fire. Realizing that the joke had gone awry, they tried to care for Wiley on their own, but two days later realized he needed professional care. Finally, on Sunday they reported the incident to the police and Wiley was rushed to the hospital.

Wiley lingered on for two weeks, and died on June 6, 1913. Annie buried her father at Holy Hope Cemetery on June 9. She arranged and paid for the funeral. In a time when the most common mode of transportation in the west was still the horse and wagon, Annie managed to give her father a funeral procession with five automobiles, each costing Annie five dollars.

When Annie filled out the death certificate she stated that her father was white. She listed no occupation but put his age down as 76, and his father as John Box, born in England.

About the time of her father's death, the temper of society began changing. The west was becoming fashionable. High society and money were finding their way to Arizona and Oracle and the Santa Catalina Mountains became their playground. They came for holidays; they came for extended visits; some became part-time residents, and some moved permanently to this mountain village. With them they brought their money and their values.

The tough, strong pioneers that had founded and built the

west were, for the most part, of mixed heritage and cultures. The new residents had a different view. They either ignored or tolerated those of different cultural backgrounds, but they certainly didn't treat them as equals.

And, in the middle of it all there were the Neals, Annie and Curly, financial and social leaders of the village of Oracle — a well-known entrepreneur and a successful international hostess. The new citizens found they were hard to ignore as so much of the village was either owned or influenced by Curly Neal. While a façade of tolerance was established, the behaviors spoke a different story.

Accusations were made against Curly and his business practices. He was sued for cutting down too many trees in the Oracle area, and in another suit, he was denied homestead rights. Stubborn Curly fought each action and in the end it cost him his fortune.

Perhaps the most hurtful to Annie was the treatment she received from the leading citizens of Oracle. Annie and Curly, once the social leaders, who were looked to for help and guidance, were now ignored for all social events except those open to the public. They still contributed generously to the Victory Bond efforts. They continued to donate beef at Christmas for the needy, feed the hungry, and give a job to anyone who was desperate. But they were not guests at the many card parties and private dinner parties so gushingly written up in Tucson's society columns. Prejudice and racism had arrived in the golden west.

That is probably the reason Annie claimed on Wiley's death certificate that he was white. She wanted him buried in Tucson, in a popular cemetery. This might be the reason Curly referred to himself as white in his later years.

Through it all, Annie kept her sense of humor. She loved to relate the story of the persistent, traveling salesman who insisted she buy a cream to whiten her skin. Annie thought that was hysterically funny and would laugh with the energy only a big jolly woman can exhibit.

However, despite her color and the prejudices of the time, Annie was well liked and respected throughout her life. After Curly died in 1936, Annie remained at the Mountain View Hotel, the only real home she had ever known. She sold the 3N Ranch to Hubert Bowyer after Curly's death but kept the Mountain View open as a resort hotel although its days of glory were gone. All Annie had left at the end were memories.

On May 12, 1950, the *Florence Blade Tribune* announced that Annie Box Neal had died at the age of 80. At the time of Annie's death the hotel had only two guests — two old miners that Annie had allowed to stay on. She may not have been a social scion but Annie was best known for being a kind and caring individual. She was a big, happy, generous soul — the saint of the Santa Catalina Mountains.

WILLIAM BLOODGOOD TROWBRIDGE
UNKNOWN - 1941

William Trowbridge

FROM THE MOUNTAIN VIEW HOTEL REGISTER,
NOVEMBER 9, 1898

CHAPTER 4:
THE LOVER

William Trowbridge flung the letter down on his highly polished executive desk. He roundly cursed the writer, the circumstances, and, mostly the day that brought him to that hellhole called Arizona. Only now was the enormity of his misplaced trust evident. It was an incredible mistake on his part, but as he had once said to `her,' "if we do not make mistakes in this life, we don't make anything else."

He swiveled his chair to stare out at the columns of Manhattan skyscrapers standing sentinel outside his window. He had the advantage money gives, a panoramic view of the city without the noise and smells. He was well insulated from such mundane things, cocooned in his executive office above the city.

His sumptuous office befitted an official of the Vermilye Company, one of Wall Street's oldest banking houses. The mantle of financial executive set comfortably on William. He never questioned his executive status; his father had been the firm's senior member for a number of years. His grandfather had been the President of the Second National Bank of New York, and one of his ancestors was a New York pioneer who helped found the St. Nicholas Society.

But he wasn't thinking of his good fortune now, nor did he see the columns of concrete buildings surrounding him. He was back in 1898 and on the hunting trip that sent him on the path of his ill-fated journey. He remembered the three days of shooting in upper New York State that almost ended with him and his companions burning down the lean-to.

His companions, Walter Wood and Ben C. Fincke, had boundless enthusiasm for hunting. But even they were discouraged and were in risk of bagging no more than colds on this particular jaunt. Fincke suggested they try the game in his home state of Ohio, but that proved to be uneventful. Then Walter had a brilliant idea. He was an attorney whose time was his own and he spent it rather leisurely. Fincke and Wood had heard of a little place in the wilds of Arizona Territory that abounded with antelope and deer, "and wouldn't it be good fun to try our hand at it."

He had initially protested. All he had with him was a small duffel bag packed with a few clothes. The bag was the type used for carrying mail and in fact he had acquired it for a very reasonable price from a government cutter carrying mail to European bound steamers.

He had learned frugality from the cradle. When he was a child, his father had insisted he keep strict accounting of his allowance, detailing every penny spent, held and received. That mindset was so imbued in him that he was constantly cautioning others to watch their expenditures. Even his letters to her had been filled with financial advice and references to money.

However, his companions had other thoughts. They weren't going to let a small bag stop them from a great adventure. They headed for Chicago on a shopping trip that ended with the trio being outfitted in the latest Teddy Roosevelt Rough Rider gear. They also got William a bigger bag.

It was Election Day, November 1898 when they arrived in Tucson, Arizona Territory. Their final destination was the tiny town of Oracle in the Santa Catalina Mountains. They managed to get rooms for the night in the Orndorff Hotel. It was Tucson's finest. The rooms were narrow and small but efficiently suited out. The next morning they started for Oracle in one of William Neal's stage buggies.

The following weeks were some of the happiest he had ever spent. If only the weather had been miserable, or the hunting poor. If only his companions were a little less pleasant then perhaps he would never have returned to the mountain village.

But he remembered enjoying the rough and good life, which included plentiful hunting, wild terrain for riding, beautiful vistas, and Annie Neal's bountiful meals. The three wore their Rough Rider clothes, had their beards trimmed on Neal's front porch and generally led a carefree life.

How he hated leaving that idyllic lifestyle, but there were responsibilities back in New York. However, Walter and Ben wanted one last memory. He suggested heading home by way of Coronado to "eat strawberries on Christmas Day beside the ocean and Santa Barbara." They did.

If he had never gone on the Arizona trip, he grimly thought, then there would not have been Katherine, or Margaret, or any letters. But the thought of a life that empty chilled him more than any winter scene could.

What had started out as a weekend hunting trip in 1898 for William Trowbridge lasted four months. In that time, the West and Oracle had captured him. For the rest of his life, he was to spend part of each year in the mountain village. It was there that he felt in charge of his life. It was there that he left his mark in generous contributions of buildings and charitable acts. And, it was there his problems started.

Over the following years, he returned to Oracle at least once a year, staying at the Mountain View and spending his days hunting and riding. He grew to love the oak-studded hills strewn with huge, dark brown, granite boulders spewed from volcanoes long dead. The weather was a blessing, a refuge from the winters that served up windy cold caverns in Manhattan and a frozen Saranac Lake countryside.

When the Triangle L Ranch in Oracle went up for sale in 1924, Trowbridge immediately bought it. The town had grown considerably since he first saw it in 1898. Now there were over 500 people living in Oracle, which included a general store, a bar, two hotels, and some fine homes such as Mrs. Steward's two-story mansion.

He bought the ranch from William Ladd; William had acquired the ranch and its rangeland from his brother's widow, Mrs. Westry Ladd. Although it was William who sold the ranch to Trowbridge, Mrs. Westry Ladd's mark was everywhere. She was from the family that produced the Baldwin locomotive engine and the ranch reflected her privileged life. The wooden floors were covered with Navajo rugs, the furniture was comfortable and much of it was antique pieces.

The focal point in the ranch house was a 360-degree adobe fireplace that defined the living room and the dining room. The fireplace was situated so it divided the two rooms with openings on both sides. A piano was tucked into a corner of the living room.

The ranch was being run as a cattle and dude ranch when Trowbridge bought it. Trowbridge knew Mrs. Meta Jones Tutt the manager. He knew her daughter Katherine better and spent considerable time with her when he was in Oracle. Her sister Dorothy said everyone knew they were "partially engaged."

Katherine had tuberculosis. Her illness was the reason the Tutts had left Atlanta, Georgia in 1921 for the healthier climate of Arizona. Perhaps it was Katherine's delicateness that drew Trowbridge, he was always attracted by those who seemed to need him. Whatever it was, he soon found himself involved with this "will-o-the-wisp."

In the late twenties, the Triangle L Ranch was considered one of the best dude ranches in Arizona. Mrs. Tutt's Southern cooking and charm made the ranch a popular destination; Trowbridge's money allowed her to keep it that way.

But that all ended four years later. In 1928, William B. Trowbridge married Miss Catherine Smith of Edinburgh, Scotland. Miss Smith had been traveling in the US when

World War I broke out in 1915. She never returned home. The marriage took place at the Natural Bridge Lodge in Arizona with the service conducted by Rev. Henry Mckenzie of the Miami Community Church. The attendants were from Natural Bridge.

It seems strange that William Trowbridge, son of one of New York's wealthiest families, had taken one of the biggest steps of his life over 2,000 miles from his home without family or friends in attendance. There is no information on how, where or when William met Catherine. Was this marriage another example of William's soft heart, in this case for a woman estranged from her homeland and family? Over the years of their marriage and their visits to Oracle, no answers emerged.

Shortly after Mr. & Mrs. Trowbridge took up residence at the Triangle L, Mrs. Tutt and her daughters left for the Dragoon Mountains in southern Arizona. With William's help, the Tutt's purchased the Triangle T ranch there for Katherine. Some say he did it to settle a breach of promise suit. Katherine died at the Dragoon ranch in 1934, her mother in 1935.

It was about this time that Trowbridge's life took a decided turn. Sometime before the summer of 1935, Trowbridge met his Margaret in Tucson. He was immensely attracted to the divorcee and he soon set up a rendezvous with Margaret. Catherine Trowbridge was not well and the necessary shopping in Tucson was beyond her strength. So twice a week William went into town. It was during these shopping trips he managed to meet with Margaret near the VA hospital, under the large tree by the black tower, well away from the downtown and prying eyes.

On July 18, 1935, Trowbridge scratched a penciled note to Margaret telling her of his travel plans. He advised her that he and his wife would be leaving that Friday on the 11:17

a.m. train for New York City. If she saw just the LaSalle parked outside the train station between 8:45 and 10:15 (10:30 at the latest) she was to take a stroll through the ticket office and baggage room. If she saw the Cadillac or both cars he warned her to "keep away."

He thought they might be able to spend a half-hour together before he left. He asked her to come as early as she could. In case they missed connections at the train station, Trowbridge listed his schedule for that morning which included stops at the Apache Buick Garage and Litts Drug Store. Ever mindful, he cautioned her to "watch out for company."

It had rained in Oracle the night before and Trowbridge wondered if Tucson had gotten any of the rain. He was concerned that Margaret might venture out in bad weather.

In case they could not meet, he wished Margaret good luck and said goodbye. But he cautioned her to keep her eyes and ears open and to send him a report in two days.

By late summer, Trowbridge was in New York and had begun a correspondence with Margaret that was to continue for over six months.

On July 22, Trowbridge wrote Margaret that he had reached his destination, but didn't like it. The weather was "… humid and you could almost squeeze the water out of it." He missed Arizona with its blue sky, dry air and wonderful nights.

He was disappointed he hadn't seen Margaret before he left, but he did have a moment of memory. The last he saw of the town from the train window was the black water tower near the Veteran's Hospital. He encouraged her to write soon and not to be too long about it, as he was anxious to hear from her.

Trowbridge reminded Margaret what she was to do with

the letters he wrote her as there were "some people not so far away from her" that would like to have the letters. He told her to keep her eyes and ears open and report all she found out. At the time, he didn't realize his concerns were more prophetic than paranoid. He signed the letter "Yours Truly," then went on to remark that although it seemed very cold and formal if she would just think about it a minute it said much.

On July 24, Trowbridge did a little shopping in New York City. At Walter & Company on Broadway he purchased a 17-jewel ribbon watch for $38.25 and had it sent out to Margaret. His letter, written the same day, told her he had searched the city to find what she wanted. He complimented her on her good taste, telling her that it was the latest as gold jewelry was coming back in fashion and watches were round again, not square or rectangle.

Trowbridge was obviously a restless and impatient man. Having left Arizona only days before he complained about the heat and rain in the city. He missed the cool nights in the desert. He repeated the saying: "all things come to him who waits and if you have patience you will have all things," but he also stated that you sometimes want what you want when you want it.

Again he warned Margaret about hanging on to the letters. He had written her four and was concerned about their disposal. He wrote Margaret that if she did hang onto them then "all your chances of my doing anything more for you will end if you keep them so we will both lose out."

The Trowbridges owned a camp near Saranac Lake, NY at a place called Paul Smiths. Trowbridge and his wife were often there when they were on the East Coast. When he was at the lake, all communication with Margaret ceased. He had no private and secure place to hide his or her letters. However, whenever he had an opportunity to return to the city he would get a letter off to Margaret.

He was miserable when he could not receive or send letters. He missed her and wanted to be with her and "... it does not seem to me to matter who knows it — excepting that family of yours who want to make something out of it." He couldn't keep his mind off of her and was afraid somebody noticed.

Margaret had appealed to Trowbridge for some financial help. He readily agreed, insisting that was what a friend was for, and she knew she was more than that to him. He promised to send her a check the next day and every month so that she could take her units. Apparently Margaret was taking some course of instruction.

Before Trowbridge left his Arizona ranch, one of the Barker boys who had been working for him, asked for a loan to set up a wood carving room. Catherine was against him giving money to anyone. After he made the loan, Catherine was so angry she refused to go to dinner with him. Instead she stayed at the ranch and went through his checkbooks while he was gone. She noticed all the cash checks and when Trowbridge came back from dinner she confronted him with the accusation "Who are you supporting in Tucson?"

Trowbridge came up with a plausible excuse, he paid most bills with cash, but Catherine was not altogether appeased. She was furious and told him she was going to New York and he could get a divorce. Things cooled down later but, as he told Margaret, they were not the same.

Trowbridge was becoming more enamored with Margaret and although he now trusted her "wholly and entirely" he felt that she could still be taken off her guard and "all unknowingly be made the tool of others to wreck both our happiness." Again he cautioned her to beware for he was positive that "what has happened before will be tried again."

Apparently someone in Margaret's family had previously threatened to expose their relationship and had been appeased in some way, probably financially.

Trowbridge ends this letter with a reference to "Billy," which coincidentally was his family nickname. Here he asked if "Billy was lonely and if he was fat enough to eat?" He wanted to know if she loved Billy, "very, very, very much" and assured her that "Billy loves you very, very, very much- if he could only tell you so." He enclosed a check, told her to deposit it and signed the letter, "Truly Yours."

Trowbridge wrote Margaret that he would be leaving the city soon and for her to keep writing but to send it regular mail and it would be held for him at his club, the Union League on Park Avenue. He wrote that while in the city, he had again done some shopping for her and was sending her three pairs of stockings, all the same color, from Lord and Taylor.

He also enclosed a gift for her to wear as a reminder. He thought the object was "cute" and for her to look at it and say "MY" which would do for the two of them.

Trowbridge was still having trouble with his wife. He felt his life was "a good deal like living over a volcano that may burst into flame at any moment." He tells of one eruption when after a prolonged silence she said "I know just what you have been doing in Tucson this winter and I am not going back until I am well enough to do my own marketing in town twice a week."

While Trowbridge didn't think Catherine really knew anything, he did believe it all came from Oracle gossip which was started by that "dear sister" of Margaret's.

Trowbridge was missing Margaret more each day and worried over where it would take them if they kept on, and where it would end and how. Wanting to reassure Margaret,

Trowbridge wrote that the money would continue, the only problem being how to get it to her without Catherine becoming suspicious.

He must have found ways because gifts and checks continued going to Margaret. She had her teeth fixed and Trowbridge probably paid for that. He told her they were lovely and wanted her to take care of them. Margaret had requested a suitcase, but Trowbridge was not happy with the selections he had seen. He waited, but then ended up buying her not one, but several. One of the cases he picked could be used for more than an overnight trip. But he cautioned her on who she went away with "as I don't want to lose you again. Have you forgotten?" he wrote.

When a tan Hudson went by the window he was writing at, he interrupted his thoughts to write "Be still my heart for what memories does it awake and when shall we meet again." He asked Margaret to copy the words of "Forgotten" and send them along with a small picture of herself. He thought he could safely keep it in his pocket.

Trowbridge lamented the fact that it did not seem to be "out of sight, out of mind" for him but rather "distance makes the heart grow fonder."

Trowbridge was preparing to motor up from the city to the camp at Saranac Lake. He sorely missed the quiet of the woods after the noise and humidity of the city. He preferred the desert, the woods and the ocean, and quoted these lines from Lord Byron to Margaret so she would understand his feelings:

> "O that the desert were my dwelling place with one fair spirit
> for my minister,
> That I might all forget the human race in loving only her —
> Ye elements, do I err in deeming such a do inhabit many a spot,
> Though numbered with their being rarely be our lot."

Trowbridge was leaving the city for a few weeks and saw no point in Margaret sending the mail any way but by ordinary post. "Save the pennies," he advised "for he only who can save pennies, can save pounds or dollars and while you know I am not stingy, I like to make things go as far as they will and waste nothing."

In one letter, Trowbridge remarked that they seem to often think of the same things. Then went on to write "… but that little word prevents so much and there is nothing we can do about it that I can see just now." (Could that little word have been married?)

Margaret had received the stockings and while Trowbridge admitted they were not exactly what he wanted to get, he did think they would be useful. "And, you know that those who do get stockings for girls always have the privilege of putting them on the girls themselves — how about it dear?" he asked.

He had sent Margaret a bracelet, one he thought was cute. He was sending her another one as a companion piece, and he assured her the second bracelet would solve the riddle of the inscription '15005EU,' which appeared on the first. He told her to think of Roman numerals to solve the puzzle. The clever inscription translated to "I Love You."

Margaret worried about the number of females accessible to Trowbridge. He agreed that there were a lot of pretty girls around the country in very abbreviated bathing clothes but assured Margaret she need not worry, he wasn't interested in any of them.

In the middle of the month, Trowbridge wrote Margaret a newsy letter. He called Friday "our day," and told her he had gotten her letters and loved them. He went on to tell her of his upcoming trip with three men. They were going fishing and sailing on his brother's schooner. That trip almost ended in disaster due to horrible weather conditions. The high winds ripped through the sails but the schooner was able to make port by engine.

The day before, he had stopped in at Lord and Taylor and asked them to send folders of the fall styles. He again sent her stockings although he really wanted to send her a dress but felt it was out of his line. He enclosed a check for her next month's school bill. He wanted her to deposit it pronto so it would arrive at the office along with the other vouchers he had sent her.

Margaret said she needed a tire; he thought she had bought one, but asked if she would have enough left over from the two checks to "squeeze a new tire out of it." He requested her to render an accounting on the state of her finances.

Margaret's letters were filled with sweet words. Trowbridge was so pleased with the last paragraph of one of her letters that he wanted to cut it out and save it. He expressed regret that he would have to burn them, as he did all her letters.

The letter with the second bracelet and a fifty-dollar check was slow in getting to Margaret. At the end of the month, Trowbridge wrote his concern about the delay, and worried about the possibility of the letter being intercepted. "I don't want it to fall into anyone else's hands but it looks very much as if someone has snitched it from you."

He would have to fret over the fate of the letter for a month. He was leaving in an hour for the north and would receive no correspondence until he returned to the city.

Deepening the intrigue that clandestine lovers sometimes weave, he suggested she get a regular hotel post card, address it to the post office in the village of Paul Smiths, NY, and write a small "+" on the card if she had not received the letter and an "O" if she had, but no other writing.

Just to put her mind at ease he wanted her to know he had not forgotten her, surely he stated, you know "that you can trust me to do as I say and I will, and I now know I can trust you." With that declaration he signed off saying if he missed the train there would be ____ to pay.

At the end of September, the Trowbridges returned to the Lake for three weeks. William thought they would head west after they returned to the city. William was concerned Margaret's letters would not be delivered to him before he left for Tucson and would be forwarded, thus arriving at his ranch in Oracle. He told her not to write after the 20th of the month. When he knew the date of his return, he would send a postcard with the message "leaving" and the date. He would sign it "XYZ."

He felt safe at this time but was still concerned about their connection. "If your family (brother and sister and her so-called husband also some of that Lubock Texas crowd like that man I told you about last year) come around for money, and should (they) see Mrs. T and were refused money don't you see that they could spill the beans as they all seem to have heard of you and me being together before and would use that as a lever to pry out some coin."

He told Margaret if that happened, Mrs. T would not stop short of a complete showdown. Although Margaret's family had vanished, he believed they would turn up after his return and pursue the same tactics as before. What those tactics were is never explained.

Trowbridge was always concerned with Margaret's health. She complained about a pain in her breast, and while he told her not to worry, he did urge her to see the best doctor she knew if it continued.

William was truly torn with obligations and emotions. He wrote of his traditional values and his dilemma. He told

Margaret that "Mrs. T's condition and state of mind are the very reasons why I should stick by her and try to do more for her and less for you because doing things for you is the very thing that makes her worse at this particular time. I have a heart" he continued, "if I did not have you would not love me, and she (Catherine) has no one but me in the whole world to turn to. Her health is very bad and at best she has not so very long to live so you can not blame me for not wanting to grieve her and further upset her state of mind. Surely you can see the difficulty I am in and will help me out all you can. If she was only well and strong and had lots of friends in this country, things might be very different."

Trowbridge was worried about the Oracle gossip and wanted Margaret to "sound out" some of the Oracle people. He suggested Archie R. (that could have been Archie Ramsey). He hoped the talk was about Margaret's sister and asked if Cook had married her again. He wanted to get something on them to use in self-defense.

Trowbridge left New York City and headed back to the Lake. Catherine had threatened to leave the mountains and come to the city if he didn't return immediately as the weather was vile and she was unhappy.

Trowbridge received his bank statement from Tucson. Although he was still urging Margaret to record her expenses, he agreed it would be unsafe for her to send her accounting to him in New York. However, he wanted her to keep it and show it to him someday. He thought it was a good thing for her to know where her money went and how she spent it. He told her, his Dad always used to make him keep an accounting of all the money he received, how it was spent, and what he had left. And it had to balance!

In Tucson, Margaret received a postcard marked October 18. The postcard of Saranac Lake read: "Expect to leave here on the 22. There's a long, long trail a winding. XYZ"

Trowbridge never made that deadline. He was back in New York City at the end of the month. He remarked that things had quieted down. He wanted to know if she had received the first dress and if it fit. As to further shopping, well his wife was doing her shopping in the stores and he was "scared to death that I may run into her if I do my shopping for you."

There must have been some hints from Margaret about marrying someone. In one of his letters Trowbridge wrote that he hoped she would "keep on loving him enough not to get married again."

Still no date for return had been set by the end of the month. Trowbridge was getting anxious. He also was getting extremely cautious. He told Margaret that they would have to be more careful. He lamented the fact that he felt someone was watching him and trying to make something of their meetings. "If we could both be perfectly natural and not in a hurry to get away somewhere and that we could have all the time we wanted together, like human beings, and not like some wild animals that someone is out to track."

December 2, and still, Trowbridge was on the East Coast. Margaret had sent him a letter and a Thanksgiving wish. He had planned on sending her some stockings, but couldn't get into the stores alone. He had sent Margaret a suit and told her that would have to do for his Christmas present, as he couldn't get away from his wife to shop.

Things had settled down with Catherine until Thanksgiving evening. Coming back from a dinner party, Catherine exploded. She wanted to know about the "postal" and again asked whom he was giving money to in Tucson. Trowbridge was beginning to believe that someone at the bank, seeing Margaret's name on one of his checks had "spilled the beans."

Trowbridge was planning on being back in Oracle at the ranch for Christmas but would be busy getting ready for the holiday and would not be alone in town so doubted he would be able to see Margaret.

In a letter postmarked December 12, Trowbridge sounded optimistic about returning to Oracle within the week. However he didn't hold out much hope of seeing Margaret, as he believed he would be closely watched. He was looking forward to the sunshine again and "the sunshine of your smile would help a whole lot to disperse the many stormy days both without and within that I have had since we parted."

He shared with Margaret his thoughts on Christmas, writing " I think Christmas is meant mostly for the kiddies and those most in need of help; they seem to rejoice most when helped."

Trowbridge came up with a plan to possibly meet with Margaret. Again, the scheming of secret lovers. If he was alone in Tucson he would park his car beyond Van's as near to 11:00 a.m. as possible. If possible, he told her to stick a note between the seat cushions and the back of the seat giving the time they could meet. But, he warned, "leave note only if car is parked near Van's."

Trowbridge did get back to Oracle for Christmas, but whatever his dreams were with Margaret they were soon shattered. In a letter postmarked two days before Christmas, Trowbridge wanted to know why she had sent her father to the ranch. It was only through sheer luck that Trowbridge was away from the house and met Margaret's father on the road. He did not tell Trowbridge what he wanted but made some unpleasant insinuations. Trowbridge was annoyed with Margaret. He had told her he would see her when possible. However, he had just received a telegram that his mother was dying and was on his way back East.

Trowbridge wanted Margaret to tell him how her father had read all his letters, letters she had promised to burn. At this point, a very hurt and disillusioned Trowbridge wrote, "thought I could trust you if no one else."

He requested she write and explain everything fully, and if his letters were to be read by her family it was impossible for him to write to her or do anything more for her. That letter was signed simply, "W.B.T."

The day after Christmas Trowbridge wrote to Margaret's father from NY. He demanded Margaret write and explain herself what "it was all about" and then he would help her out if she needed help. Trowbridge saw no reason for Margaret's father to become involved. He said it would do no good for any of them to go to the Oracle ranch, as there was no one there. However, if he preferred, he could see Trowbridge's lawyer, Mr. B.C. Hill. But before anything could be done, Trowbridge wanted to see or hear from Margaret.

Margaret responded with two letters. They shattered Trowbridge. "It is hard to have to say," he wrote, "that I have lost all faith in human nature now, for I did trust you as you well know." Twice before Margaret had behaved in an unacceptable manner and Trowbridge felt this time, the third time, was too much for him.

Trowbridge wrote her "what you say about me being responsible is quite impossible for several reasons which I cannot write." He believed it was a plot hatched by her father with her as a willing or unwilling partner.

Margaret's father had the letters and wanted to return them to Trowbridge in person, but it would be some time before Trowbridge returned to Arizona. Trowbridge suggested a third party in the person of any lawyer who will keep things as quiet as Margaret wished. One who would act for him and see that he had proper protection for anything he gave to her. He wanted it settled once and for all.

Trowbridge believed he and Margaret could have settled any misunderstanding before her father had entered the picture, therefore, he wanted the father to state his case plainly and quickly as he could settle things better from New York now than any future time in Oracle.

Since Trowbridge was taking a trip in a few weeks, he would not be able to communicate with Margaret or her father. He wanted Margaret's father to state what he wanted and if he agreed, and if the letters were sent back to him, he would promise to get her the money promptly.

If Margaret's family did not like his proposal, then his lawyer would handle the situation and, Trowbridge warned, "this would mean a long, drawn out fight which cannot be helped and will be advertised."

On January 17, Margaret received a letter from Trowbridge stating that what she wrote about was "quite impossible for several very good reasons that could easily be shown but would require a lot of investigation, but it could be done." He felt he had always helped her in the past and been fair with her and did much for her during the summer. If she wanted to play fair with him, he requested she send him the hospital bill duly certified by the hospital staff, and all of his letters, then he would send Margaret the money. But he would acknowledge no responsibility for her being ill. First he wanted the letters returned by insured or registered mail.

The next month, the last of Trowbridge's and Margaret's correspondence arrived. He acknowledged receipt of her letter and telegram, and stated it was impossible for them to reach any agreement for the amount she requested. To raise such an amount he would have to sacrifice something, and it would soon become known throughout the office, and brought to the attention of his family.

If it were to become public then he would thrash it out in court, as he would not pay out the amount Margaret requested without a court decision settling, once and for all, the question Margaret had raised.

If Margaret persisted in this demand, he threatened to hire the best lawyers he could and lay things wide open. If she won a decision in the lower court, he would carry it to the highest court of the land.

Trowbridge wrote that if she had been more honest with him, if she had said she needed some cash, and that she did not think his wife would want to see the letters he had written, he would have been a good enough sport to be a good loser. Trowbridge had saved $5,000 in a Tucson bank over the summer and he would have been willing to turn it over to Margaret and call it square. "But the other that you try to make me believe ... Oh, no."

His postscript told her that "under no circumstances" was she to send any more telegrams as they would not be received. Now that she had accomplished her purpose, Trowbridge did not believe she would care about sending him letters. This would probably be the last time he would ever write to her. "I am really sorry that events have shaped themselves that it should have this kind of an ending."

There were two more letters in the packet of Trowbridge's and Margaret's correspondence. In April, 1936, M.L.B wrote to W.B.T.: "When you come in town Monday 12 or Tuesday 13 whichever day you come in on, I must see you about sompthing very important. Something that you must know, and right away. Drive to the east end of the Broadway Subway at 1 p.m. o'clock. I will wait for you there, both Monday and Tuesday — Everything will be OK. If you fail to show up I shall go to Oracle to see you. That is how urgent it is. So be sure and be here. Excuse Printing, M.L.B."

That month, Margaret received the following letter: "Dear Margrette, I got your letter today, glad you got the letter, do hope you get news soon that he is back ou boy do I, margrette I have been thinking that you will be sick along about the 12 or sooner and I am a way over hear if there is a school close to you where I can send Bettie to school I will come and stay with you until you get sick. Lucile could stay with Loreta I shure would like to be there until you are sick, I will come if you and Paul want me to if I can send Bettie to school there and if you want me to come. You could let me no some way Sat. Loreta is coming up and I could come back with her. It would save extra expenses for the treap you could send me a wire if you want me to no by Sat what you think about it. I have the bans made 6 of them well I will close. Mother."

The letter from Margaret's mother was the last correspondence in this mysterious packet. This relationship between Margaret and William in the summer and fall of 1935 was documented by over two dozen pieces of correspondence found over fifty years later in an abandoned well at the Triangle L Ranch. While they tell of the relationship, they pose more questions than they answer.

What was the important news Margaret wanted to tell Trowbridge? Did it have anything to do with the illness that was referred to in several letters? And, was this news that Margaret was pregnant? What did Trowbridge mean when he wrote the accusations were impossible and he could prove it, although it would take time and investigation? Was Margaret's family accusing him of impregnating Margaret, and was he sterile? Did Margaret give birth to Trowbridge's child? Did he buy the letters from the family? Is that why the letters were on Triangle L property? And, when and who deposited the letters in the well?

If Trowbridge did receive the letters from Margaret or her

family, it seems strange that he would keep them after his many requests that Margaret burn them. And if he was burning her letters to him, why would he hold on to these incriminating ones? Perhaps Trowbridge never did receive the letters. The family could have demanded money from Catherine Trowbridge for the letters. Catherine could have thrown the letters away in the well thinking they were safe there. Then again, maybe she kept them in the house and when her doctor inherited the property, he found them and disposed of them in the well.

The well was no longer in use when the letters were put there. They were not in a waterproof container, nor is there any sign of water damage on any of the envelopes or letters.

And so the mystery remains. What happened to end the relationship between Margaret and William Trowbridge so acrimoniously, and where did the letters come from? Who put them in the well?

Was Trowbridge a young man who had been given wealth but had never received love? Was he nothing more than a means to money for most people? Had any woman cared more for the man and less for the bank account? Or did he use his wealth to impress and get his way?

Although William Trowbridge remains an enigma, something can be told about him from his letters. It seems the very wealthy Trowbridge was extremely frugal. He constantly wrote about counting pennies, and the importance of keeping accurate accounts. Yet, he gave generously to projects in Tucson and Oracle. And he never denied Margaret her wishes. He built the first schoolhouse in Oracle, donated money to the Tucson Y and contributed land to the University of Arizona for soil experiments.

At times, his letters were peppered with trite sayings, other times he quoted famous poets and writers. He was almost silly at times with his love statements, and at other times was a practical and cautious man.

It was rumored he had affairs, and these letters seem to be proof he did. However, he felt a great deal of responsibility towards his wife, and wanted to protect her.

It is said Catherine was older than Trowbridge, and it is suspected she came from a lower class family. Her snobbery toward others could have easily covered a sense of insecurity about her birth. She held tightly to her precious social status. And, while socially accepted, she was not well liked by the people of Oracle. She was a small woman with a big temper. She demanded total attention and was somewhat of a hypochondriac. She was known as a curt and insulting woman. Yet, she left generous sums of money to her ranch staff and to the small Oracle stone church. She never spoke of her husband or her marriage after Trowbridge's death.

Trowbridge made the statement to Margaret that his wife was sick and probably would not last more than a couple of years. Ironically, she outlived him by twenty years.

Trowbridge died unexpectedly in 1941. When his will was probated it was worth over a million dollars. He left Catherine $10,000, Oracle property and a yearly sum. She returned to New York for her summers, staying at the Plaza Hotel, but the Triangle L Ranch was her permanent home.

Catherine is buried in a small cemetery in Oracle. William B. Trowbridge is buried in New York, far from his beloved Arizona. However, some say that on certain evenings there is a spirit that wanders at the Triangle L. It is a sorrowful and lonesome spirit and those who meet it are left with the feeling that it is a kindly soul, seeking love.

ELIZABETH LAMBERT WOOD
1871 - 1962

Elizabeth Lambert Wood with her son, Lambert, age 6   Oracle Historical Society

FROM THE MOUNTAIN VIEW HOTEL REGISTER,
JANUARY 19, 1902

CHAPTER 5:
THE MOTHER

My beloved Arizona sun warms my eighty-three year old bones as I sit on my patio pouring over my diaries and papers. I have left the paper work until the very last. It is a painful process as it brings some distressing memories to life.

I am closing out my Arizona life and returning to my family in Portland. Yet, my heart will always be in Oracle. It was here Dr. William Wood and I spent so many happy days. Here my children grew to adulthood. These bits of paper and diaries around me reflect my fears, joys, heartbreaks, and yes, even the anxieties of my Arizona life, a life that started on a January morning almost sixty years ago.

We came to Oracle for Dr. Wood's health. He had tuberculosis and his doctors held no hope for him in the cold, wet climate of Oregon. The doctors suggested New Mexico.

We left our daughter Helen and our son Lambert with my sister and moved to Albuquerque. I was emotionally torn. I sorely missed the children; yet I knew it was important I go with Dr. Wood. He was physically incapable of caring for himself.

We rented a cottage from two elderly sisters in a quiet country area. At first things went well. I enjoyed the small neighborhood we lived in and the daily walks in the countryside. Dr. Wood gained some color and several pounds. However, in the fall when the chilly winds came off the mountains, Dr. Wood became increasingly weaker.

We had heard about a small village in the mountains of the Arizona territory near Tucson. The village called Oracle, was reporting remarkable results in the cure and care of consumptive patients. We decided it was best if Dr. Wood initially went out on his own. I stayed in Albuquerque to clean our rented cabin and say goodbye to our new friends. Shortly after Dr. Wood left, I received a letter overflowing with enthusiasm for Arizona and ordering me to come immediately.

I booked my train ticket for January 6 and could hardly wait. It had been hard to leave the children behind, and now alone without Dr. Wood, my days in New Mexico became a succession of lonesome, hollow hours.

What an adventure that trip turned out to be. My train was over six hours late arriving in Tucson. By the time it puffed into the station it was midnight, I was tired, sooty and I ached from the uncomfortable seats. The train station was nothing more than a small platform next to an even smaller wooden building with the grand name of the San Xavier Hotel.

As exhausted as I was from the difficult journey, I was filled with joy at seeing Dr. Wood waiting for me, although I thought him too thin. Together we headed for our room at the Orndorff Hotel, a somewhat larger and grander building a few blocks away.

The next morning, I left Dr. Wood sitting in the sunshine and walked to the Parkview Hotel to place a call to Mrs. William Neal, the proprietress of the Mountain View Hotel in Oracle. As I walked to the Parkview, I was taken by the looming, yet beautiful Santa Catalina Mountains that bordered Tucson on the north. Knowing our destination was to be a small village in the northwest of these mountains filled me with excitement. I was anxious to start.

We set out the next morning at six o'clock on the Neal Stage, the only transportation available other than one's own horse. The trip lasted six hours but was broken by a stop to change horses at Marin's ranch, twelve miles outside Tucson. Mr. Neal maintained this abandoned ranch as a stage coach station. After a brief rest, we headed out on the most arduous part of our trip. It seemed to be straight up on a dusty dirt trail overgrown with cacti and alive with rattlesnakes and wild game. We spied deer in the distance and caught coyote slinking away in the brush. Hours later, as we topped the Oracle ridge I began to see signs of the village.

Over a mesa covered with cat claw and cholla, we had a straight-on view of beautiful oak and grass woodlands. Moments later, we came to the impressive red brick Mountain View Hotel. It glowed like a jewel in an emerald setting of green lawns and gardens. The surrounding countryside was covered with golden grass, oak and black walnut trees. As we pulled into the hotel yard, Annie Neal was there to give us a warm welcome and to supervise the unpacking of our huge pile of luggage.

Baggage disposed of, Mrs. Neal escorted us into the colorful interior of the hotel. She led us through the large reception area, up the stairs and into another large hallway. Following behind with our hand baggage was Choppo, an elderly Mexican man. Our room faced southwest and from one of our windows we had a magnificent view of the mountains. The French doors opened onto a wide verandah inviting us to walk out and enjoy the grand view.

It was love at first sight for me. I knew I wanted to spend the rest of my life in this wondrous land. I sensed that living here would bring me opportunities I would never be offered anyplace else. The mountains seem to beckon me to come explore them, to discover their secrets. I vowed then that I would do my utmost to become part of this land. I thought of the fun that I would have recording my adventures and that day, I began my Oracle Diary.

Elizabeth stared thoughtfully off at her beloved mountain, then with great effort, she leaned forward and took the top diary from the pile on the slatted table in front of her. Carefully she flipped through the yellowed pages spotted by time and weather. Randomly she stopped and read a page here and there.

1902
January

Dr. Wood and I have been riding every day scouting out this impressive countryside. No matter in what direction we ride, or look there is a breathtaking view. I have been using a sidesaddle Mr. Neal found in the barn. It hasn't been used in a long time and the leather is dusty and cracked in spots.

We were curious about the mining in Mammoth and decided to ride in that direction today. As we approached we could see it was alive with activity. The miners are working full out to supply the 20 stamp mill three miles away on the San Pedro. You can feel the earth shake miles before you reach the stamp mill — a steady fumd, fumd, fumd. We saw Mr. Neal's twenty-horse ore wagons piled high with the rich ore heading for the mill. These wagons have the most enormous wheels, which are needed to transport the weight of the ore.

On the way home, a miner directed us to a shortcut. Dr. Wood took off on his horse Billie and I found myself alone on a steep grade heading toward a narrow trail. As my horse and I plodded along, the trail disintegrated to a narrow ledge. The drop was steep and my feet were hanging over the sides. There is no place to go on a sidesaddle. I felt suspended in mid-air, a feeling that terrified me. Dr. Wood was well ahead and there was no one in sound or sight to help me. I only had my pounding heart for company. I imagined all sorts of terrifying events: my horse would stumble, the ledge would give way and I would slide off the decrepit sidesaddle. I couldn't turn around as the ledge was too narrow.

Fortunately, my horse Joe was better at climbing mountains than I was. He soon had me on wider and more level ground. That was enough. When I returned to the hotel, I begged for a regular saddle.

1902
February

I sometimes forget how untamed this country is. Today Dr.

Wood and I had a reminder. We were riding after a band of antelope, an exercise we find entertaining and exhilarating, when we met Joe Castro. He is the best vaquero and a top roper at the 3N Ranch. He was riding near the Represa, an area named for its small dam, when two men emerged from the bush, one on each side of him. One asked for a match as his hand shot out to grab the bit on Castro's horse. Before the man had the bit, Joe Castro's pistol was pointed at them. He shouted for them to get out and leave quickly. Joe and his pistol must have convinced the men as they scurried off. We learned this afternoon that the two men had escaped from a deputy sheriff and were headed for Mexico.

1902
March

We rode up to the Burgess Camp in the Old Hat Gulch with Dr. Scudder another Mountain View guest.

Captain Burgess, owner of the camp, is a former Army scout. On one of his prospecting trips, Captain Burgess lost an eye when he was ambushed on the trail. Since that time his married daughter has accompanied him on his trips armed with a heavy-bore rifle and a shotgun. Charlie Jackson is the caretaker at Burgess Camp. He is a tall good-natured Negro and makes the best dried apricot and peach pies in the world. Charlie and Dr. Scudder took to each other immediately. When we got back to the hotel, Dr. Scudder borrowed my Spanish dictionary and renamed the camp calling it Campo Bonito. He is seriously thinking of buying the property.

1902
October

Dr. Wood and I are back again in Oracle after a summer in Portland. I enjoyed being with my family but I found my thoughts returning more and more frequently to Oracle and the Santa Catalina Mountains. This place has captured me in ways I never would have suspected. I longed for the strong winds playing with the trees, the heady smell of creosote after a rain, the rainbows that invariable follow a monsoon downpour, and most of all the beautiful land and our horseback explorations.

We returned with the children. I could not bear to be away from them any longer. We are staying in the Neal's redwood, gabled cottage across from the hotel. It is a lovely two-bedroom cottage with magnificent views of the mountains. I have spoken to Mrs. Estill and she has agreed to school Helen and Lambert in her home along with her children. Mr. Estill owns Oracle's one and only store. There is a school in Oracle, but I want the children to be free to travel with Dr. Wood and me.

1903
February

There have been some very heavy thunderstorms. The kerosene lamps and Coleman stoves do not provide enough light and heat for Dr. Wood. I have him bundled up and huddled around the Coleman. We must purchase a generator; he can not tolerate the damp and cold. Old timers say they have not seen rain like this in over a generation. Every wash is running with soil; vaqueros and horses are bogging down in the silt and soggy sand.

Everyone is tired of staying indoors so the sight of a sunny day yesterday was enough to encourage some of the Mountain View guests to plan a javelina hunt in the foothills of the Galiuro Mountains. A local Mexican lion hunter agreed to act as guide. They had asked Isreal, a cook from Atlanta, Georgia, to go along, but he opted to stay in his camp. In what I think was an act of desperation, they asked if I would like to accompany them on the hunt as their cook. Dr. Wood and I joined the group and we headed to the Southern Belle mine to pick up Charlie Brajovich, the caretaker at the mine and an excellent camp cook. It took some convincing, as Charlie was sure we were in for the biggest storm of the winter. We could see Apache Peak was already buried in black clouds.

The storm caught us before we reached the canyon. Charlie hunkered down and rode for the Crooked G Ranch and the two-room adobe of Jesús Castro in Old Hat Gulch. Bolts of lightening struck the ground around us. We found out later that three horses in Oracle were killed by the storm.

With Charlie leading the way, we finally reached the Castro adobe. Jesús must have seen our approach and he rushed out to help us. His petite wife, Guadalupe, pushed him aside to help me off my horse and into the house. As we dashed into the house, we were greeted with the aroma of freshly baked, yeast bread. Two loaves and two-pounds of butter sat on the table permeating the cabin with their delicious smells. In my sopping condition, a dry house was a blessing; the homemade bread was a miracle.

Guadalupe put the coffee pot on the stove then took me into the next room. She lit a miner's candle, pushed the point into the adobe wall and set about drying my hair with a towel. It wasn't long before this tiny woman had taken matters into her own hands and I was reasonable dry and we were all being treated to fresh bread, butter and coffee.

1906
May

We have spent the past six months in the most idyllic of places. Mr. and Mrs. Chauncy Buzan invited our family to visit Trains End Ranch in Aravaipa Canyon. We took the children on horseback. We were somewhat concerned as the ride is 40 miles and I was sure it would tire them. However, when we arrived they had more than enough energy to run and play in the mountain stream that was high from the snows off Mount Graham. I was so proud of them. They did very well for their ten and eight years.

We had left some camping equipment from our previous visits, and the Buzen's allowed us to occupy a cabin on the upper end of the ranch. We made many trips to the lesser known parts of the Galiuro Mountains. It brought me so much pleasure, seeing the children discover the wonders of the Arizona wilds. On one ride, we spotted several longhorn sheep. Lambert wanted to chase them but we discouraged that by promising him he could ride on cattle if we spotted any. Helen was more impressed with the wild flowers and the baby cactus wren we found. Another time, we spotted a bear and were sure to stay clear of his territory. We left most of our equipment in the cabin and plan to go back every few months. The children were genuinely sorry to leave the Galiuro Mountains.

1907

September

Here you never know what adventure will greet you tomorrow. We have just had one of those unpredictable adventures. Indian Joe has been working for Mrs. Steward for several years. She is one of the grander Oracle residents having retired here with her flour-manufacturing husband several years ago. He has since died, but she remained in their Oracle mansion home which is filled with fine European artwork.

Indian Joe was given permission to live off the San Carlos Apache Reservation and has been a good worker and no trouble, at least until last night. Every fall the Apaches are given permission by reservation authorities to come into Oracle and harvest the bellotas, the sweet black oak acorn. Yesterday, about a hundred Apaches arrived and made camp at Cherry Valley.

We were sound asleep in the middle of the night when the most piercing yells and screams ripped through the air. The four of us tumbled out of our beds and rushed outside where we stood paralyzed with fear and in a state of total confusion. William Neal rushed by with a big rifle in his hand headed toward Apache Joe's rancheria. We were soon told to go back to bed, the situation was well in hand.

Today a sad Indian Joe and his family were marched back to the reservation along with the other Apaches. "Tiswin" cost him his privilege of living off the reservation. His San Carlos friends had brought a supply of Tiswin with them. This potent drink is made by soaking corn in water then fermenting it by simmering the brew over low coals. It is strong enough to blow the top off a volcano and Indian Joe's head.

1908
February

The three of us have returned to Oracle after another summer in Portland. Lambert is not with us. He now needs more schooling than Mrs. Estill can give him. Sadly, we have left him in Oregon at the Portland Academy. Helen is still with us, but it will not be many more years before we must seek more schooling for her. We still ride daily and take several of Helen's school friends along. I must enjoy her while I can.

Dr. Wood has decided that we will come back to Oracle around Armistice Day every year and stay until the Portland weather is warm enough for him to return for a visit. If only my family and our business interests were here. It would make for a simpler life. Dr. Wood's condition makes it impossible for him to practice his skills as an oculist so we must continually return to Portland to help with the family banking business.

We have decided to move out of the Gable cottage and move deeper into the Santa Catalina Mountains. Charlie Brajevich's adobe in the Old Hat Gulch District suits us perfectly. The house is surrounded by fruit trees planted by a former owner who had great ideas for an orchard. He didn't succeed, but the trees did.

1908
September

Spring and Fall are roundups times around Oracle. Dr. Wood and I have seen many a cattle drive run through the village, but I have never been on any of the roundups. When Herbert Bowyer told us there would be one held in the Cañada del Oro, we decided to go along as spectators.

We reached the American Flag Ranch as dawn was breaking. The vaqueros were gathered around the fire enjoying last cups of coffee. Tony Feliz was one of the roundup crew. He had his half-breed hounds with him to aid in the gathering of the cattle.

I stationed myself on a high point where I could view the activities all around. I could hear the cattle bawling, and, occasionally a deep bay from one of the dogs. I spotted a flash of red charging through the bush and saw that one of Tony's dogs was hanging on the nose of a steer. The dog's feet were splayed to grab onto the ground when possible. The job of the dogs is to slow down the cattle so that some rider can rope, throw and brand the animal.

The vaqueros are amazing ropers. Tony Feliz, Joe Castro and Charlie Moss are among the tops. I was riding not far from Charlie when Feliz barreled by with a big steer on the end of his rope. Right in front of Charlie, Feliz's riata broke. Without any noticeable arm movement or thought, Charlie's loop shot out at the same time his horse shot forward, the rope circled and tightened on the big steer's neck and the animal came to an abrupt halt. That was the quickest piece of roping I have ever witnessed.

1909
April

This year started out with sadness. My father died in Portland. We managed to get to Portland to see him one last time and he died shortly after our arrival. He and mother had been married over 45 years. She was rather listless and preoccupied when we left. My sisters and brothers are near at hand and I know they will help her over this painful time. The grandchildren seem to cheer her and she will be living near many of them.

Father was the founder of the Citizen's Bank in the city and remained president until the day he died. Both father and mother were very active in Portland and I know her many friends are there for her.

When I returned I found the mountains helped my pain. Their strength and mystic comforted me.

1910
February

"Buffalo Bill Cody" is in Oracle. He and Mrs. Cody came to the Mountain View last night. William Neal, the owner of the Mountain View, was a scout for Buffalo Bill and they have remained friends. Buffalo Bill asked me if I would visit with his wife at the hotel where she is staying while he camps out at his mine in Campo Bonito. The mining site is too primitive for Mrs. Cody.

They are a contrasting couple. He is tall, flamboyant and very energetic. She is small and quietly pleasant. She has a motherly look about her. She is a comforting sort who would rather sit on the porch knitting than go riding around the countryside. She is a very unpretentious person. I spent a number of enjoyable hours with her.

She confided a great secret to me. Buffalo Bill's long white hair is a wig. We spent the day talking of many things, one of which was Cody's interest in gold mines. She preferred raising hogs and growing alfalfa to mining claims. At one point, she was winding her wool onto a small metal object. One of the male guests asked her what it was. She unraveled the wool enough to show the piece. It was Cody's Medal of Honor. I expressed concern over the treatment of such valuable objects. I pointed to the saddle with its silver embossed buffalo heads that Queen Victoria had given Cody. It was lying on its side on the ground. She told me they had so many valuable things they had no place to put them in their North Platte ranch. To her they were only "negligible trifles."

1911
October

George Acton and his family invited us on a quail hunt. We planned to use his empty tufa-block house on the east bank of the San Pedro as a base. He and his family have built a new dwelling on the west bank. The weather refused to cooperate today and the downpour turned the river into a swirling mass. We were anxious to join the Acton's on the other bank and decided to forge the river. One of George's older boys rode ahead of us. The pony had been trained to shuffle his feet in the river. This action pricked the bubbles of water that create quicksand on the river bottom.

We followed the Acton boy into the muddy torrent. I was having trouble keeping my horse's head up and was losing ground to the angry river. All of a sudden, my horse Joe plunged ahead. Charlie Brajovich had given him a healthy punch on the rump. That action cost Charlie control of his horse and he was thrown into the river on the downstream side. His horse was soon out of reach, plummeting head over heels downstream.

Mrs. Acton ran to a bend in the river. She was able to get a rope around the horse's neck, which helped the horse plant his feet on solid ground. The horse stood there, muddy water running out of its nostrils, ears and eyes. Meanwhile, George was able to get a rope to Charlie who was being bounced around by the swirling water. Charlie was pulled to the opposite side of the river, barely alive. He lost 30 pounds in that adventure.

1912
February

We heard today that Arizona has been admitted into the Union. It is the forty-eighth state of our great union. I don't really know what I expected would happen when this historical news was announced, but I must admit I was surprised when nothing happened. It became merely a topic of discussion at our social events. Frank Daily believed it would mean more rules and restrictions for the ranchers. Terry thought it might make it easier for him to receive goods for his store. Some of the miners thought there might be more money for mine development. However, I think Neil Kannally summed it up when he said, "You never know what the government will do, so there is no point in speculating." All, however, are concerned about how much control the government will try to maintain over the state. We in Arizona are independent people, use to self-governing and self-politics. Time will tell. People around Oracle are more interested in the price of beef and the latest rainfall than what people are saying and doing almost two thousand miles away.

1914
August

Dr. Wood and I are alone in Oracle. Lambert is at Williams College in Massachusetts finishing his last two years. Helen is enrolled in St. Helen's Hall in Portland. It is the Episcopal

School for girls that I attended and graduated from in 1890. Between my sisters and my nieces it seems there is always a Lambert in attendance. We will visit her next month and she will be with us for the holidays.

1917
November

America is now in the European war. We are so proud of Lambert. He graduated from Williams College in Mass. And after completing his training in Plattsburg, New York, was commissioned a Second Lieutenant in the Army. He was able to come home for two weeks and we spent our time riding and visiting friends. I look at him and he is a man, no longer the child I worried about with skinned knees and torn pants. My worries now are more fearsome.

1918
January

I have received a letter from Lambert. He has been assigned to the Ninth Infantry, Second Division. I am torn between pride and fear. As any mother, I worry about his safety, but as any parent I am so proud of his patriotism and courage. Dr. Wood and I are still riding in the morning. There are times when I spot a particular site that Lambert loved and I miss him so much it is like a physical pain.

1918
March

What a busy year I have had. In the beginning of last year, I was asked to set up a Red Cross shop in Portland, patterned after the ones in New Zealand and Australia. We opened the shop in late August. It was the first of its kind in the United States. By the end of the year we had added two large buildings, a salvage store and a wholesale department. It is a resounding success, by Armistice Day we cleared over $50,000. I think my experience as a writer and my contacts in the world of newspaper advertising helped the shop. I have left it with my assistants and have returned to Oracle.

1918
July

I received the telegram last week. Lambert was killed in action southeast of Soissons, France on July 18 while commanding the Machine Gun Company of his infantry division. He was awarded the Distinguished Service Cross and the Croix de Guerre for his courage and bravery. I do not think my heart will ever be whole again. He was only 23. Dr. Wood has been very silent since we received the news. I worry about him for he is not eating much and has been brooding. I do not know what to do. He has always loved it here in Oracle, but nothing interests him now.

1921
September

We are living in Charlie Brajevich's three-room lumber cabin. The setting is quiet, and the views are magnificent. This is perhaps our most favorite spot in the Oracle mountains. Dr. Wood seems to be more content, but still introspective.

While the cabin is on Charlie's land, the garage is on Southern Belle mine property. I hadn't thought too much about that until this afternoon. I went into Tucson to do my weekly shopping and met our attorney John B. Wright. He told me the Southern Belle was up for sale. Mrs. Coddington, the owner, inherited the property but has no interest in the mine. She is selling her American holdings and settling in Paris, France. I was so excited I drove our 1920 Model T back to Charlie's at top speed, which is 20 miles an hour. I couldn't wait to tell Dr. Wood. He met me as I drove up. I excitedly explained my meeting with John Wright, but Dr. Wood was not interested and would not consider purchasing this property. He commented that the sale of the Southern Belle should not affect us. I had cold chills thinking of where we would go when the property was sold. The idea of tearing up roots and leaving with a sick husband makes my blood run cold.

1921
September

I cannot let it rest. I was awake most of the night figuring out how much of my own money I had and what I could afford for the property. I felt I really needed some advice. The person I immediately thought of was Mary Kannally, my very dear friend at the KAN Ranch. She said she would talk to her brother Neil to get his opinion. I can not wait to hear his reply. Meanwhile I am checking over my personal finances to see how much money I have available.

1921
September

I saw Mary today and she told me Neil said I should buy the property. He considers it a good investment. I told her I would offer three-quarters of the price Mr. Wright named. "No, no." she said, "Offer only half the price." I am nervous about that idea but will do it. Tomorrow I'm returning to Tucson to see Mr. Wright. I have some other legal business with him and I plan to make my offer at the conclusion of my meeting.

1921
September

I met with Mr. Wright today. I concluded my legal business and as I was leaving turned and told him I was interested in the Southern Belle. I stated my price in a casual manner, almost as an afterthought. He was horrified, announcing it was too low, but said he would send the offer to Mrs. Coddington.

1921
October

I can not really believe Mrs. Coddington accepted. I am now the owner of the Southern Belle property which has a patented mine. The deed also includes the Morning Star mine. I fretted over telling Dr. Wood. He had shown no interest in the property. But when I told him what I had done, he gave me a long look then burst out laughing. He thought it was a good joke on him and was rather proud of me.

1921
December

We had a surprise visit this week from Mrs. Young. Mr. Menager of Tucson brought her up to see the mine she had discovered. She is an interesting and charming woman and I spent the day hearing about the discovery of the Southern Belle mine. It is a fascinating story.

Mrs. Young came to what was called Granite Ranch as a bride. She would bake pies and take them as part of her husband's lunch to his Imperial mine in the Canyon which was on a ridge in back of their home.

One day, she started out early walking up the steep incline that went around Mogul Peak. When she reached the gap where the trail to Oracle goes over the ridge she turned onto the path to the Imperial mine site. Halfway there, she sat down to rest. Without thinking, she picked at the surrounding ridge with a hairpin she had removed from her hair. She absent-mindedly flaked away at a whitish vein streaking through the ledge. She loosened several dull yellow rocks, and shaking with excitement wrapped them in her husband's handkerchief and rushed up to the Imperial, totally forgetting her husband's lunch pail.

Mr. Young could hardly believe what she had. They quickly returned, almost running down the ridge. With a pick, he uncovered larger and richer pieces. In the end, they discovered one of the richest veins of gold in the area. Mr. Young named the mine after his wife, a southern belle. The Youngs had nothing so when Ed Fellows offered them $1,500 in cash for the Southern Belle claim they immediately agreed. It is estimated the Southern Belle eventually yielded over half a million dollars in gold. Later on, Mr. Fellows purchased a block of twelve claims including the Morning Star and added them to the Southern Belle property. Mrs. Young told us she had returned because she dreamed she had found another mine. Sadly that never happened.

1922
March

Since acquiring the Southern Belle property in the Old Hat District of Pinal County, we are spending most of our year here in Oracle. The weather is so much better for Dr. Wood. Although he has not gained a lot of weight, he is holding what he has. His coughing spells have lessened but he still seems to be despondent. I try to get him out riding once a day, but he is less and less inclined. At times he seems so far away. A few friends came over for a picnic, but even that did not seem to cheer him

1923
August

Dr. Wood died in July of this year. His disease and the despondency were more than he could cope with. I feel I have failed him, although I do not know what I could have, or should have done. His will to live gave out, and he ended his pain. I buried him in our family plot in Portland and came back to Oracle.

The Southern Belle was too big, and filled with too many memories for me, so I have moved to what was Castro's Crooked G Ranch. It came to me with the Southern Belle property. It is a lovely, peaceful spot in Peppersauce Canyon. There is a large spring running by a natural grove of sycamores, black walnuts and ash trees. I have saved the white columbine seeds from the flowers growing on the creek bank and scattered them around. It is a magnificent sight when they are in bloom.

With the Castro ranch, comes the privilege of running some cattle and horses. What a joy it is to see my brand, a bell with a horizontal S as its handle. I hired Ramón Ronquillo and his brother to tend the cattle. They are hard workers, but very poor.

1924
September

Helen is married. She and her husband Alexander Randall live in Philadelphia with my brand new grandson. How I wish they were closer. I am planning a trip to Philadelphia in the next few months. I am excited about seeing my grandson. Hopefully I can be of some help to Helen. She has not completely recovered from the birth.

1925
February

There is quite a bit of excitement here in Oracle. Hollywood has arrived. They are filming *The Mine with the Iron Door*. The author, Harold Bell Wright, was a health seeker who became fascinated by the legend of a hidden mine in the Santa Catalinas. He was at the Mountain View trying to recuperate when Dr. Wood and I were there. He was so ill he could do little but lie in the sunshine. Eventually, he moved to the far reaches of George Wilson's Linda Vista ranch. He claimed he needed the solitude for his writing.

The movie company is using a few local vaqueros as extras. They are filming scenes at the Linda Vista Ranch and all over Oracle. Some of the buildings in the village were given new movie names. The Terry store now has a big sign proclaiming it the Oracle Store. Ray Hotton, of the Linda Vista, got annoyed by some of the changes. In defiance, he painted the Linda Vista brand in white on all the horses the movie company is using. The director smiled at this defiance, but left the brands.

1925
July

Helen was not recovering from her illness. Alexander thought a trip to Europe would cheer her up as she has been moody and depressed. Unfortunately, her depression was more than she could bear and on their way back to American, she drowned. I have been taking care of her son since he was six-months old. I have now adopted my grandson and given him my son's name. Lambert and I are living in Peppersauce together. It seems strange at 44 to be a mother again, but these are days I consider precious and will hold them dear to my heart. Lambert is a good baby and brings me great joy.

1925
September

This morning my gift window to the United Church was sanctified. It was a lovely service and gave me a great measure of peace. It was a cloudy morning, but as we sang the final hymn the sun peaked through the stained glass and I felt at that moment that Dr. Wood, my son and my daughter were there with me.

1926
March

I am appalled at the lack of playground space for our school children. I have been pondering this problem for a few months and decided that a mesquite thicket up from the Acadia Ranch Hotel would be an ideal location for a playground. To this end, I purchased two 1.66 acre parcels. I had the ground cleared and a merry-go-round and a baseball diamond with a backstop built. It was a happy occasion when we opened the playground to the children. Their laughter bounced off the Santa Catalinas.

The playground was dedicated on Armistice Day. Rev. E.C. Clark officiated. Mrs. Graham and Mrs. Stille, teachers from the Oracle school, were also there. The town has honored me by calling the playground Wood Field.

1929
November

Oracle put on its annual Indian Pageant last night. We held it in the park, in a hollow where the main village road turns toward Cherry Valley. We parked our cars on the hill overlooking the hollow and turned on our lights. We lit up the area like a stage. We were able to get some Indians to come from New Mexico and Flagstaff, but we didn't have enough. We used local boys to add to the tribe. Unfortunately, the weather was cold and the gunny sack outfits we made for our local boys offered little protection from the wind. We tried to make them look authentic by painting their bodies. Mike Muñoz, one of the children, complained loudly every time they dipped the brush into the bucket and rubbed it on his skin. I thought he looked and sounded like the real thing.

1930
September

This summer I was invited to visit France with other gold star mothers. On August 25, Mrs. Claudia Muse, Mrs. Anita Burruel and I left Tucson as part of the Gold Star Pilgrimage. The following two weeks brought me great comfort and joy. We toured the battle sectors in France, Germany and Belgium. The trip was beautifully planned, I am still amazed over all we saw and did.

1931
February

I drilled for water near the playground. The townspeople all pitched in and we struck water at 38 feet then again at 42 feet. Now, Oracle has a major well for its use. The town men cribbed it with cedar and put in a hand pump. It also has a trough for the livestock and you can always find wild donkeys or a milk cow or two with their heads in the trough. The well gets plenty of use. Few houses in Oracle have their own water supply. Those with wells share the water, but some of the wells are too far away to make the fetching of water an easy task. This new well will help and be more accessible to both people and animals.

1931
September

Lambert came home covered in chalk dust. When I asked him what had happened he merely said, "The County School Superintendent said that we were the worst school in the county; we didn't want to disappoint him." I thought it best to go down to the school and get the story from the teachers. As it turned out, it was more mischief than not.

It seems Joe Felix had roughed up one of the boys. Although the teacher did not approve, she privately admitted that the child had it coming as he was continually pestering Joe. Joe picked up the bully and shook him. The child was a Pierson and today Mr. Pierson came up into the schoolhouse wearing a big black hat clear down to his ears. His boots were laying over on the side and he stormed into the room cussing. The teacher tried to get him to go outside into the yard with her. She didn't want the children to hear the language. He replied, "Hell no, I ain't going outside." She then asked him to take off his hat and he replied, "Hell no, I won't take my hat off." Of course she was completely distraught, but finally convinced him to go out into the schoolyard with her to discuss the problem.

Apparently, while she was outside, the boys started an eraser fight. They energetically powdered the girls and each other. When the teacher returned to the classroom and saw the mess she announced that all would be punished. She instructed the students to line up and take their licks with the paddle. When she came to Hugh McClue, who was rather chunky, she had to use two hands. Hugh's bib overalls were loaded with chalk dust. Hugh's punishment produced a large white cloud that covered the classroom.

1932
March

Oracle finally has a golf course. Tad Lynch, who works for the county, Horace Smith and Vince Killerlane and one of our teachers decided they knew how to play golf and that what the town needed was a golf course.

The County furnished a little bit of the work but most of it was hand labor by the local lads. The number one tee is about two miles from the Acadia. The number nine hole is also there. It is all on Neal's property but he does not seem to mind and has not asked for any fees.

The fairway is only probably 50 to 70 feet wide and there is a lot of brush out there. You shoot across and then climb the hill and shoot down the hill to the flat. It is about 127 yards. They screened sand to a certain size then mixed it with used motor oil. This produced a greenish soil that they used for the greens. It makes for a strange golf course, but it is nine holes.

It has turned out to be a benefit to some of the local boys. They are earning extra money caddying. For some, it is as much as two dollars a week. It is very welcome, as most of the families are poor and there are so few ways to earn extra money.

1933
May

The rock church is truly a community church for Oracle. During the week, the school uses it for the children. On Sunday, the Catholics use it first thing in the morning and it is busy all day long with other services. It has a lovely pipe organ and Lambert has the responsibility of cranking it. He sits on a little stool and has become an expert on just how hard to crank and at what pace. I can't help but smile when I see him so intent on his job. He takes it quite seriously.

I turned my two-year-old car over to the schoolteacher. I buy a new car every other year and give the old one to the teachers. On their pay, they cannot afford to buy their own car. They are such dedicated souls. It makes their life easier having transportation.

1935
January

I have returned to my heart here in Oracle. I left Peppersauce two years ago and planned to be back in a year but travels kept me from returning until now. How homesick I was for Arizona and Peppersauce. Even so, I managed to be very productive. I wrote 42 travel letters and a children's story. All of them were published in Oregon.

1938
April

Southern Belle Ranch is such a lovely setting, but the memories here are painful. I have been seeking a worthwhile organization that would use the land wisely and have now completed negotiations with the Salvation Army. Its new name will be Camp O'Wood. Lambert and I cannot keep up with the work, and we do not need the space. We are quite content living at the old Crooked G. The Salvation Army is thinking of using it for a children's camp.

1939
June

We now have electricity in Oracle. It is coming in from Mammoth. I'm going to buy a refrigerator for the ranch. Alan Ramsey has been trucking up a ton of ice each week for our iceboxes. It doesn't last long in the kind of heat we have been having. Emptying out the bottom tray can be a chore and if you wait too long you wind up with a flooded floor. I'll be glad to get rid of it. Another blessing is not having to depend on the generator. It is fine for emergencies but can be temperamental.

1941
December

Another war has darkened our country. I prayed we would never see the return of the horrors experienced during the Great War. I want to keep all our young men here at home, and protect the families from the heartbreak war can bring. But all I can do is pray that it will end quickly and our youth and families will be preserved. Our sons should enjoy growing into adults and living their full lives, but I am afraid it will not be. The news is ominous. And so I pray.

1942
October

Oracle is without its young men. They are in the service. Lambert has been gone many months now and is in pilot training with the Army Air Corps. An eastern consortium of two brothers has asked to lease out my mine, the Morning Star. Apparently there is tungsten there and it is vital to the war effort.

1943
February

There is nothing more heartbreaking than to be a mother who has lost a child, unless it is to be a mother who has lost all her children. This thought pounded in my mind as I lay to rest my only grandchild. He has joined my husband, son and daughter in what I hope is a more peaceful life with God. Like his namesake, my son, he was killed in action fighting for our country. I cannot believe that life could be so cruel to me. I refuse to think I do not have a role, a meaning to my life. I must go on, I must spend my days trying to find that meaning, to bring some happiness and joy to others, and thus I hope some peace to myself.

1945
February

The children of Oracle have so little. To bring some extra joy to their lives, I have been having special parties for them here at the ranch. On Halloween, they came and dunked apples and heard ghost stories around a fire. We all roasted weenies. I gave each a bag of candy to take home. Christmas time Mrs. Ramsey, Mrs. Trowbridge, Mrs. Wilson and I planned a special party for them. We had them out here and gave each a present of some clothes. Archie Ramsey dressed as Santa Claus. One of the smaller children was so awestruck she broke out in tears and went running to her father at Mr. Ramsey's "ho ho ho." The children sang carols to the adults and our hearts swelled with pride and nostalgia. The ranchers gave each family a piece of beef for their Christmas dinner.

1945
March

It is Easter; the days are going so fast. I organized an egg hunt for the children. Several of the women helped me dye eggs in bright colors. The men hid them around the ranch, however, Mother Nature did not cooperate. It snowed 18 inches at night and the eggs are impossible to find. We made it up to the children with games and songs.

1945
April

We found the Easter eggs. As the snow melted, patches of bright color appeared. Although the colors ran, the children inform me the eggs are still good as they have been refrigerated. It certainly is a colorful sight on the ranch with splashes of green, yellow, red and blue appearing randomly around the property.

1947
January

Driving is getting more and more difficult for me. I have decided to hire a chauffeur. Young John Ronquillo has been doing odd jobs for me and I thought he would make a good driver. I asked him to take me into Tucson a few weeks ago and he did a fine job. Imagine my surprise when I found out he didn't have a license. I told him I would hire him as my driver if he got a license. It took him three trips to Florence but he finally passed. I pay him fifty cents a day for driving me around and doing odd jobs on the ranch. For a young lad of 16 that is quite a windfall.

1948
September

To make birthdays special for the Oracle children, I give them a party on their day. Today was Alice's birthday. She is eight. I picked her up after school and brought her and her friends to the ranch. There were a few small presents here for her and a big cake. The wealth from the tungsten lease is well spent in bringing these simple pleasures to the children. It brings me great joy when I see them smile.

1949
June

Some of my most poignant memories were made here at the Crooked G ranch, but I now find that at 78 years life here is more than I can handle. I am going to donate the ranch to the Tucson YMCA. It is my hope they will turn it into a summer camp for young men. It will be called the Triangle Y ranch.

1951
November

Oracle has a famous visitor. Jane Russell, the movie actress, is visiting the Linda Vista. *Look* magazine was there to take several pictures of her near the stream in the Cañada del Oro. I am looking forward to seeing the magazine when it comes out.

Miss Russell is not the first famous guest of the Linda Vista. In 1947, Thomas Dewey was a special guest of George Wilson. George is a staunch Republican and invited Dewey to visit the Ranch. Dewey was the Republican Presidential candidate and was regarded as a shoo-in for the office. I spent a pleasant evening at the Linda Vista with this distinguished gentleman.

Of course, Buffalo Bill was a frequent visitor to the Mountain View Hotel when he owned mines here. But not all our distinctive visitors have been honorable. In 1938, John Dillinger and several of his mob came into Newt's Bar. Apparently they were looking for some out-of-the-way place to relax and have a few drinks. Dillinger and his men returned to the city that evening. A few days later, he was arrested in Tucson.

1953
May

I have just come back from a week in the mountains. The solitude helps my writing. Ramón Ronquillo goes with me and we camp out. While I write, he sees to the horses and the cooking. He is an excellent companion and leaves me to my writing. I am writing down my memories of the fascinating characters that have lived or wandered this area. I don't think anything will ever match the wit, wisdom and cunning of the original territorialists, and I want to preserve their stories.

*   *   *

Elizabeth Lambert Wood spent her final years in Portland, Oregon, surrounded by her family. From time to time she corresponded with Edith Stratton Kitt, Secretary of the Arizona Pioneers, answering questions on Arizona's pioneer history.

Elizabeth left Oracle a legacy of love and caring. She donated a number of properties to be used for the health and happiness of children. Among them were the YMCA Camp and the Salvation Army property, both located in Peppersauce Canyon. To the town of Oracle she gave, over her lifetime, a number of gifts including the village well, the children's playground, the stained glass window in the stone church, and the legend of Mother Wood.

GEORGE STONE WILSON
1887 - 1957

George Stone Wilson   Arizona Cattlelog

George S. Wilson

FROM THE MOUNTAIN VIEW HOTEL REGISTER,
MAY 2, 1906

CHAPTER 6:
THE COWBOY

George was a problem. Oh he wasn't bad; he was mischievous. He wasn't mean; he was a jokester. And, he wasn't incorrigible; he was stubborn. Oh, was he stubborn! It was the combination of these traits that finally brought his downfall at Phillips Exeter Academy in New Hampshire. The staff at Exeter expected proper behavior from their young gentlemen students. After all, the academy was one of the most prestigious boys' schools in the United States.

Administrators and staff took seriously their mission of teaching young men proper manners and values. Among these values were honesty, politeness and social graces. So it really went against their principles when George and his cousin were caught cheating on a test. They expelled both boys.

Tom thought they should confess. "Look George, we admit to the act, they cane us, we wail — loudly — and all is forgiven."

George wasn't at all enthused about that plan. He wasn't about to admit to anything. Tom tried his best to convince his cousin of the merits of his plan, but George was unmovable. He stubbornly refused to confess.

Tom confessed, received his obligatory blows, wailed loudly, and was reinstated. George remained silent, stubborn and expelled. It didn't help matters that George had irked a teacher only days before. The man had written a problem on the board. Standing in front of the class, pointer in hand, he asked the students where he should put the pointer. A very obliging George told him.

The combination of George's "misdemeanors" was too much for George's father. George's mother had died when he was twelve years old and poor Thomas Hudson Wilson couldn't seem to control his 19 year old son. The senior Wilson decided the best thing for his only son was to send him off. Perhaps on his own, George would learn responsibility and discipline, not to mention honesty.

George was tall and lean. His nose was a bit too obvious for him to be called handsome, but he made up for that with copious charm. He had a sharp sense of humor and you had to really listen to him to catch on to his quips.

Although George was a fine athlete, he did suffer from asthma. He had recently torn a ligament near his lung, and that too, was bothering him. Keeping these in mind, the senior Mr. Wilson began his search for a place for George. From a fellow Chamber of Commerce member he heard of a new health resort in the Arizona Territory. That seemed far enough away to teach George the lessons he needed to learn. He wired Mrs. Annie Neal, the proprietress at the Mountain View Hotel, and made arrangements for George.

In April, 1906, a teenage George was placed on a westbound train with a stern warning not to have anything to do with strangers. George, being the way he was, stopped in Chicago for a few days to take in a baseball game. He loved the game and played it very well. Of course, the first thing he did at the ballpark was to take up with the stranger sitting next to him. It wasn't until the stranger was walking George to his hotel that he remembered his father's warning. George was lucky on this one. The stranger got George safely to his hotel, and advised him to stay in and not go out that evening. For once, George listened.

When he arrived in Tucson, he was met at his hotel by William Neal, owner of the stage coach line that would take him to the Mountain View Hotel. Neal informed George that the stage would pick him up at six a.m. the next day.

He woke at five and was waiting in front of the hotel by six looking quite spectacular in his city clothes and derby hat. In fact they were his only clothes. The railroad had misplaced all of his luggage.

The coach arrived promptly at six, barreling down the road heading straight for George. At the last minute, the driver pulled the brake and the stage came to a screeching halt. Curious about these unknown and strange lands, George decided to ride outside with the driver. Two old miners took inside seats. There was a small window in back of the driver so George could talk to the miners, however for the first part of the trip, they had little to say.

Twelve miles from Tucson the stage stopped for a change of horses at Marin Station. About this time, the miners loosened up enough to ask George where he was going. He told them Oracle and they promised to introduce him to the Chief of Police and Chief of the Fire Department. George was impressed that he would meet such notable people on his first day.

Several horse changes and six hours plus later, George Stone Wilson arrived at the Mountain View Hotel. As the stage pulled into the front yard of the hotel, the guests came hurrying out to greet George. For a young man so far away from home, the greeting seemed a warm act of kindness that managed to calm some of his anxieties.

The stage changed horses and continued the trip to Mammoth with the two miners aboard. George realized the miners never introduced him to the town officials. Looking around him George could see why the introductions were not forthcoming. The "town" of Oracle consisted of two hotels, the Estill store, the Estill home and the Steward house. There were about a half dozen peripheral ranches including Neal's 3N. But nothing of them could be seen even though there was enough cattle from these ranches roaming free all over the "town" including some in the hotel yard. If everyone in town held an official position there still would be enough titles left over to appoint a few cows and horses. The sudden feeling of isolation that washed over George almost staggered him.

George made quite an impression on the hotel staff. Next to his name in the hotel register were the following comments: "kid," "terrific dopis," "state of innocence," and a slang expression of the times "Sportibus."

Shortly after he arrived, George wandered out to the cattle corrals where the steers were being separated from the cows and calves for market. Leaning on the rail, he was enthralled with the action in the corral. Neal was the only man inside the corral on foot. Bowyer, the ranch foreman, yelled at Neal to get along the fence, as some of the steers were mean. These words were no sooner spoken than Neal came racing toward the fence followed by a nasty steer chewing at his rear end. Neal flung himself at the fence. Unfortunately, George had been so fascinated with the action, he didn't realize Neal was headed straight for him. Both went hurling to the ground with Neal on top of George and both on top of the derby. That was the last derby hat George ever owned.

Within two weeks, the novelty of being out west wore off for George. Most of the guests at the Mountain View were older except for Mr. and Mrs. Clyde Way of Mason City, Iowa (who later became his best friends.) Lonesome and homesick, he wired his father for money to come home. His father wired back that he would have to stick it out for six months. A bored George faced with an empty five and half months decided to fill his days riding with the cowboys when they worked the cattle.

What started out as time filler turned into an education on the day-to-day workings of cattle ranching. These lessons were learned mostly from the ground up. It must have been a good education because George ended up being one of the most experienced and successful cattle ranchers in southern Arizona.

George was a fairly decent rider but his cowboy skills were non-existent. Needing practice, George looked around for tamer victims to hone his skills on. Curly Neal owned over 150 goats and Annie Neal raised geese and chickens. These animals roamed freely around the hotel grounds. When Neal wasn't around, George practiced his roping on the goats. Annie Neal thought this was very funny. When Mrs. Neal wasn't around, George would run through the geese, pick one, catch it, shake it, and drop it. Of course, this entertained Curly Neal to no end. However George's practices soon had the livestock so wild no one could get near them.

George had an insatiable curiosity and that led him to some interesting adventures. One day, sitting on the Mountain View porch, he spotted Neal and Bowyer heading out in a two-wheel breaking cart. One of the goats had fallen in a mine shaft and Neal was mounting a rescue mission. Now that sounded like fun to George, so he tagged along.

The Oracle mine shaft was about 10' square and they could see the goat at the bottom. He was a big billy with wicked looking horns. The shaft was 60 feet deep with two tunnels running out from it. Neal and George gave Bowyer some candles and lowered him on a rope to the bottom of the shaft. The goat was uncooperative and Bowyer spent some time running the goat back and forth through the tunnels. Neal figured George had better go down and help him. So he lowered George down to the bottom of the shaft on the rope. Bowyer gave George a candle as it was very dark in the tunnels and told him they would both go back in the tunnel where the goat was and try to catch him by a leg. The tunnels were only about 4 feet wide and six feet high so the goat didn't have much room to escape.

George lit his candle and they started out with Bowyer in front. They went back about 20 feet from the end of the tunnel where they could see the goat's eyes, then things started to happen. That goat doubled up like a sprint runner and came down that tunnel a mile a minute. In that closed tunnel he sounded like an express train. Bowyer and George flattened themselves against the side wall as the goat went by. They followed him into the other tunnel and the same thing happened.

After chasing the goat from one tunnel to the other, Bowyer decided to change tactics and told George to stand in the mouth of one of the tunnels and he would go into the other and bring the goat out. This didn't sound like a good idea to George but he said he would try it and after a few minutes he heard that goat coming.

George braced himself and was ready to grab that goat any way he could, but the goat was too much for George. The goat butted George in the chest, knocked him down, crawled over him and got back in the tunnel.

The trio was not about to give up, but this time they decided George wouldn't try to grab the goat, but just keep him from going into the other tunnel. When George heard the Billy coming, he doubled up, covered his face with his arms and waited. When that goat saw George in the mouth of the tunnel, he jumped on George's back and tried to claw his way up the wall of the shaft.

He was still on George's back when Bowyer arrived and got hold of him by a leg. They wrestled the goat to the ground and tied his feet together. Neal, who had seen the whole performance, was so convulsed with laughter that he couldn't pull the goat out, so Bowyer and George had to sit down for a few minutes until Neal could get control. Bowyer and George cussed that goat and then they cussed Neal for thinking it was so funny as they were both scratched and bruised.

George often wondered how they would have ever got

that goat out of there without his help. At last, Neal said he was ready so they fastened the rope on the goat and Neal pulled him out. He then pulled George out, and both pulled Bowyer out. George looked at the goat and wanted to kick him in the belly for what he had done. He never liked goats after that.

Many of the Mountain View guests had their beds placed on the narrow hotel porches as fresh, night air was considered beneficial for consumptive suffers. There was no more than two feet between the bed and the porch rails. Between the cramped space and the coughing that went on all night, George got little sleep so he asked Mrs. Neal if he could have a canvas house tent built somewhere on the hotel grounds. House tents were large tents with wooden floors. Since he was a long-term guest, she agreed.

Mrs. Neal had a German carpenter that was very good when he was sober. He was, however, considered a little weird by most people. He was a tall man, well over six feet with a big raw bone build. Electricity was one of his favorite topics and he would stop what he was doing and rush into his tent saying New York or Washington was calling him. When people told him he couldn't get messages without wires, he would stare at them with disdain and inform them that you didn't need wires because the sound came through a tube in the air.

George's tent was located about a quarter mile from the hotel and George would walk there in the morning and back in the evening. An old Mexican had a tent near George. One day he showed George a set of fresh mountain lion tracks that passed between the two tents, which were about 100 yards apart. After that, George and the Mexican slept with rifles next to their cots. More than anything, George wanted to bag that lion.

One night George heard a chilling scream that raised the

hairs on his neck. Both George and the Mexican high-tailed it out of their tents clutching their rifles, but all they saw was the black of night. A few mornings after that, George was awakened at daybreak by the blast of a rifle. Racing out of his tent, he saw the Mexican, rifle in hand, standing over the dead lion. The lion was a large beast measuring at least eight feet from nose to tail tip. George deeply regretted not shooting that cat.

Contrary to George's initial expectation, life was not dull at the Mountain View. Annie Neal planned interesting and entertaining amusements. Some of them were even a trifle bazaar such as Race Days or Rodeos. These were held once a month with the venue alternating between the Acadia Ranch and the Mountain View. There were a number of events for guests and locals to participate in — including steer roping and calf tying.

For the flag race, small flags were pegged in the ground every 50 feet for a distance of about 300 feet. The rider had to lean down from his horse and pluck up the flag while riding by at hell-bent-for-leather speed. The rider that crossed the finish line with the most flags was the winner.

But the most hilarious race was the chicken pull. A chicken was buried up to its neck in the ground. The rider had to start his horse at a full gallop, pull the chicken up and get to the finish line with the chicken. Best time was the winner. Unfortunately the chickens didn't cooperate. Many of the riders who got a good grip on the chicken were parted from their horse when the chicken stayed in the ground and the horse went on. The ones that were lucky enough to get the chicken up didn't have it any easier. The chicken would flap its wings, scratch, and struggle. This, of course, spooked the horses and they would bolt for the cacti and bushes, rider, chicken and all.

Annie Neal loved to celebrate holidays in a grand way. The

July 4 celebration in 1906 was no exception. Just about everyone who was within riding distance came with his or her family. Miners, cowboys, ranchers and farmers were there for the fireworks and dance. They started celebrating as soon as they arrived so by late afternoon few were firm on their feet.

There were no fireworks regulations in 1906 and the Neals had supplied an abundance of "crackers" including pinwheels, skyrockets, giant cannons and Roman candles. After the spectacular sky show, George headed for his tent to change for the dance.

The party was in full swing when George got back to the hotel. Anyone who wasn't drunk before he left was drunk now. George was into his second dance when he heard the loud noises coming from the kitchen. Curious as ever, he went down to see for himself.

About a dozen men, including the hotel help, were trying to see who could drink the hottest beer. The beer was heated on the stove and when it was deemed hot enough some fool would down it. According to George the others pressured him into joining the contest. It only took about five minutes for George to be as drunk as the rest.

About that time, a little guy by the name of George Carpenter who worked for the Neals swaggered up to George, and told him he was going to "bust him in the nose." Since George Wilson towered over George Carpenter, he overlooked the statement. After all, when sober, George Carpenter was a nice guy and one of Wilson's best friends.

Although George was willing to overlook the threat by little George, Big Bud the waiter was not. He walked over, punched little George and knocked him down. That was all the action needed to start the "fireworks" in the kitchen. Everyone got into the melee; punches were flying in every direction. The light in the kitchen went out when the lamp was knocked over. That didn't stop the fighters. Even though it was pitch black in the kitchen, the fight continued. Men just swung at any shadow.

Neal's foreman came down from the dance floor and told everyone to get out as they were breaking up the place. Without missing a punch, the fighters brawled their way out the back door into the hotel yard.

Bowyer had left Herman Krock, one of the hotel employees, to guard the garden gate. One of the fighters picked up Herman and tossed him over the wall. Herman struggled to his feet and rapidly left saying he knew every bone in his body was broken.

Meanwhile, Annie Neal heard the commotion and came hurrying out to the yard. She charged right into the fracas, grabbing Wilson by the collar. Feeling the pull, he swung around and popped Annie on the nose. Blood spurted all over her beautiful party dress. With that, Annie sent George Carpenter and Big Bud to their rooms. Stubborn Wilson would not move. Annie ordered two cots to be brought outside. With some help they put George in one and Bowyer took the other.

The next morning a disoriented George woke up wondering where he was. As he glanced around getting his bearings he spied the leg of his best suit hanging from the wire fence that enclosed the yard.

Herman Krock fared better than most after the party, not being very brave had its compensations. But, Herman Krock had other unique character traits. He was a chicken farmer, and figured it was his business to learn as much about birds as he could. He often wondered if vulture's attacked only dead animals, or just still animals. One day, in the summer, Herman stripped down and lay out on a hill. For hours he stayed as still as possible waiting for the vultures. They never came but Herman got a free ride to the hospital. He stayed there for two weeks recuperating from severe sunburn.

It was in May, 1907 that George left the Mountain View Hotel. George's father had sent him an ultimatum; either get a job or come home. George opted for work. He had friends in Portland, Oregon so he headed there and obtained work in the lumber business. George rose through the ranks of the Inman-Poulson Lumber Mills. By 1910, he had a responsible position and a good salary. When the mill closed for six weeks in December, George went to visit his family in Binghamton, New York. One week in the cold and George made the decision to head for the warmer weather of Arizona. Accompanied by his father, the Wilsons took a leisurely route, going through Atlanta and New Orleans before heading for Tucson.

Father and son registered at the Mountain View Hotel on January 9, 1911. The weather was warm and sunny and the Wilsons' spent their time making new friends and visiting old ones. It was then that George decided he wanted to spend his life in Arizona; a few days later he told his father his decision. Mr. Wilson reminded George he had a good job and land waiting for him in Portland, and how was he going to make a living? "I'm getting into the cattle business," declared George. And he did. He sold his property in Portland, resigned from his job and took on the life of a rancher. Even though he was now a ranch owner, George still enjoyed the social life at the Mountain View.

Josie Neal, Annie and Curly's adopted daughter, was getting married. It promised to be an outstanding party. Annie had hired two bands from Tucson to play continuously which they did for 36 hours. The music didn't stop until four o'clock the next afternoon. One room was set aside just for the champagne, beer, whiskey and wine. It was self-service and the huge crowd from Oracle, Tucson and all points generously helped themselves.

George arrived for breakfast and as he was headed out the back door he ran into a group of girls up from Tucson. Archie Ramsey, the deputy sheriff, introduced George. Three months later on January 3, 1912, he married one of the young ladies, Carlotta Gonzales. It was to be the only marriage for either one. Together they established the Linda Vista Ranch and raised their sons, Thomas and Boyd, in the hardworking ranch life.

Carlotta came from a distinguished heritage. She traced her ancestry back directly to Juan José Dominguez who was one of Rivera's Leather Jackets that marched on San Diego in 1769. For his loyalty and service, he received the right to the first cattle ranch in California. When Juan José became blind in 1804, he resided with his nephew, Cristóbal Dominguez, who was in charge of the troops at the Mission of San Juan Capistrano.

When George married "Lottie," she gave up her lovely home in Tucson with all the modern city conveniences to live in an out-of-the-way mountain ranch without running water, an old wood stove and outdoor toilet.

What their ranch life lacked in conveniences it made up for in adventure and danger. Much of it was from the wildlife. One day while out riding the range, Wilson came across the camp of two old prospectors. Having just shot three rattlesnakes, they were on his mind. He asked the prospectors if they had seen any rattlers. They said the place was full of them, and about a week ago, in the Cañada del Oro near the Pusch ranch, they had had a unique experience. They and their Mexican cook had set up a campsite near an abandoned adobe building that had an old fireplace. The cook was always bragging about his fine mulligan stew, so they told him to go ahead and make it. The cook got a large pan, filled it with water and anything else he could find including meat, potatoes, beans, peas, onions, and cabbage. He set the pail on the coals in the fireplace.

When the stew was ready, three hungry men set down to dinner. That stew was as good as it was bragged to be. When they reached the bottom of the pot, however, they found the remains of a rattlesnake, rattles and all. One of the old prospectors collared the cook and was going to give him the beating of his life. The cook begged and begged and said he knew nothing of how the snake got in the stew. At this point, another snake dropped down from the chimney into the live coals. When they looked, they found the snakes had been on a ledge in the chimney and the heat had driven them off, first one in the stew, the other on the hot coals.

Not all the exciting moments came from the wildlife. Even the equipment needed on the range could be unpredictable. Most of the cowboys carried a 38- or 45-frame six-shooter. The 45-automatic was new and George had just purchased his. They were not yet perfected. Sometimes you would shoot and the gun would go off two or three times. Most of the time, however, it would clog and not go off at all.

One day George had been out on the range shooting at coyotes, rabbits and rattlers. His Mexican vaqueros were fascinated. The next morning at daybreak as they were starting out for the daily roundup, they spied a coyote on the skyline. One of the Mexicans asked to try George's new gun on the coyote. George handed over the gun and the Mexican took careful aim. The gun went off twice. This scared the Mexican and he dropped the gun to the ground. When it hit it went off again and bounced up. It kept bouncing around and every time it hit the ground it would go off. Thirty men took off in thirty different directions.

In 1922 and 1923, droughts brought the cattle industry to its knees. The Linda Vista had had no rain for almost two years. George was forced to find a way to keep his ranch going. In 1924, on the advice of Harold Bell Wright and Angue Hibbard, a friend from Chicago, he and Lottie started their guest ranch. The West was just being "discovered" by tourists from the East. Wealthy men and woman wanted the flavor of the old west without too many inconveniences. Business was so good that every year, for a number of years, George added a cottage.

George had met Harold Bell Wright, the novelist, at the Mountain View Hotel. Wright suffered from lung disease. When he first came to Oracle, he was so weak he spent his days lying on a cot where he was gently cared for by his Philippino servant. The Mountain View Hotel register shows his first visit as May 30, 1916. He signed in as Harold Bell Wright, Hollywood, Calif. July 26, he was back at the Mountain View. He came with a companion listed as Geo. Doc. Years later when Wright needed a place where he could rest and write, George offered his ranch. There at the Linda Vista Ranch, Wright penned his most famous novel.

On the furthest reaches of the Linda Vista, Harold Bell Wright and his servant set up a tent camp. Everyday Wright's servant set up his small writing desk in the fresh Santa Catalina air and Harold worked on his book. This book, *The Mine with the Iron Door*, turned into a best seller and was made into a popular movie of the times. The book was inspired by the fabled story of a rich gold mine in the Cañada del Oro, the location of the Wilson Ranch. The ranch also served as headquarters for the movie company when they filmed the story.

Wright developed some of his fictional characters from the residents of Oracle. A minor character, George Wallace, is a thinly-veiled George Wilson. The two old prospectors might have been drawn from the personality of prospector Alex McKay, the founder of Oracle. Apache Joe, who wandered in and out of the Cañada del Oro, probably inspired the character of Wright's Natachee.

Actor Bob Frazier played the part of this Indian who represented a schizoid personality of savage and cosmopolitan. Anxious to get "into character," Mr. Frazier tried to acquire an Indian-look by tanning himself in the Arizona sun. He became so burnt he was close to being serious ill. Bob spent several days in bed and shooting had to be rescheduled.

There was a doctor who lived in Oracle at this time who was incapacitated by his lung disease. He was so weak he could not practice medicine. Is he perhaps Dr. Saint Jimmy Burton of the book? Or, did Harold Bell Wright draw upon himself for this character?

George's ability to get into unique situations never abated. One of his guests, a Mr. Ray Smith, president of the A.O. Smith Corporation, flew his family to the ranch in his Belance single-engine plane. He entertained the guests by flying them in relays all over the West. However, George wasn't interested in flying. George loved to fish though, so Ray planned a fishing trip to Guaymas, Mexico. Ray and his wife, the pilot, Bud Yoakum, and George and Lottie took off. Their first stop was Nogales, Arizona, on the Mexican border, to take care of the Mexican paperwork.

It took them five hours to complete the paperwork and get permission from the Mexican authorities. During this time, a windstorm came up. George thought they would wait until the storm passed, but Ray Smith told the pilot to take off. Once airborn, they could see the roofs of houses being blown off. The plane stood on its nose, then its tail dropped, and then it shot up in the air. George expected it to hit the ground at any moment.

He wasn't sick though, just scared to death. He had a grip

on his seat that you couldn't pry loose with a crowbar. When they arrived in Guaymas the weather was beautiful and clear.

Fortunately, the trip home was uneventful. However, George's next trip in a plane was equally as exciting. They were visiting Ray and his wife in Milwaukee and were flying to a small camp in Wisconsin. After two weeks of fishing, they started their return trip. Coming into the airfield they noticed that the field was stacked with hay in piles from four-to-six feet high. They came down and almost touched the ground when the pilot gunned the engine and they shot up again.

When George asked Ed why he hadn't landed, the pilot replied the plane was going too fast. The second attempt met with the same results. Ed circled the field. On the third attempt, they shot across the field, plowed into the stacks of hay, and came to a shuttering stop. When George got out, he looked at that plane and it looked more like a 20 foot high haystack than an airplane. George decided he had had enough flying excitement for a lifetime — he never flew again.

It seems the Wilson family was destined to have terrorizing travel experiences. After visiting George at the ranch, George's father, Thomas Hudson Wilson, decided to return to New York via steamer from California. He and friends embarked on the SS President Adams. It was a lovely trip until the ship got to the coast of Panama. There the liner struck a reef off Colon. The ship had problems finding the channel and went aground while cruising full speed ahead. Fortunately, there were no casualties, and the passengers were transferred, without serious incident, to another ship and taken ashore. It took six days for another liner to arrive. Meanwhile the Wilson party was wined and dined royally by Officials of the Dollar Line. The return voyage was made to

New Orleans on January 30, and from there the party continued on to New York.

George had other talents besides cowboying. He was an outstanding baseball player and pitched for a Tucson team sponsored by Mr. Phil Brannen. Their schedule included Phoenix, Bisbee, Douglas and El Paso. When there were baseball games, the railroad ran special trains. So it was, that when Phoenix arrived to play Tucson the field was filled with Phoenix fans. Between the two teams, there were about a thousand in the stands. Phoenix was confident, and the fans were betting fast and furious on their ball players. Tucson won 10 to 2.

That called for a special celebration. George and his teammates went to the Cabinette Café. The Cabinette was a combination of dining room and bar. They had a few drinks and the celebration got a little raucous. They decided to serenade the town from the rooftop. Some music critic didn't appreciate their talent and called the police. Big Judd Arnold, the chief, arrived and he immediately recognized the choirboys. He told them to get down; they thumbed their noses at him. After considerable loud discussion, he pulled out his six-shooter and threatened to shoot them if they didn't come down. The singers thought that was funny and they had a good laugh over the threat. So the police chief did what he had to do, he shot them. But of course, he shot over their heads and as soon as they realized what the chief was doing, they commenced their singing.

Finally, in desperation, the chief said he would buy them all drinks if they got off the roof. You've never seen such a fast evacuation. They nearly broke their necks getting off that roof. George was in such a hurry, he tore his pants and Judd had to borrow a couple of hairpins from a passing lady to hold the pants together. Afterward, Judd told them he should have shot the lot and saved himself the price of the drinks.

George's life was filled with incidents like this. He brought humor to the Catalinas, a love of the land, and a dedication to the cowboy way of life. When he died in 1957, a lot of laughter was lost in Oracle.

WILLIAM FREDERICK CODY
1846 - 1917

William F. Cody "Buffalo Bill"   Private Collection

FROM THE MOUNTAIN VIEW HOTEL REGISTER,
JANUARY 15, 1909

CHAPTER 7:
THE MINE OWNER

He entered the hotel as he entered the arena — with a forceful stride, defying everything and everyone in his path. His tall, slim frame was as straight as ever, however Curly noticed the lines of time and their pull on the once proud face. The scout stood eye to eye with Annie Neal, but had to look down at the much shorter and stockier Curly.

"Curly, old Pard." He reached out and gave Neal a powerful pat on the back. His voice still had the timber to reach the far stands, but to Curly it sounded a little reedy, and maybe a little desperate. But there he stood, his white flowing beard and shoulder length hair eliminating all doubts about it being none other than "Buffalo Bill" at the Mountain View.

He was here, he told the Neals, to meet with Mr. Ward about some mining property up the road at Burgess's Campo Bonito. Did Curly know anything about it?

Not too much, Curly informed him. It was part of the Southern Belle group. Some gold, some silver and now some scheelite had been found around there. That was about all Curly knew.

"Come on up to the room. I want to talk to you about the mine with the iron door." With that bit of temptation, Cody strode off after his baggage which was hoisted on the back of a harassed and much bowed-over Mexican man.

This was Cody's first visit to his old scouting partner's hotel. Curly and Cody went back to the Indian War days, but after their scouting jobs were over, they each went their separate ways; Neal to Arizona and his business ventures, Cody to the world and show business.

In his Mountain View room, Cody stood looking out over the mountains knowing the Old Hat District was located somewhere in the canyons and hills. Through the years the Old Hat had produced mines with gold, silver, copper and scheelite (tungsten ore). Cody was planning on his new mining property being one of the producers.

A tap on the door announced the arrival of Curly. Cody, ever the congenial host, ushered him into the room and offered him a tumbler of whiskey. Cody always had a supply with him. When traveling with his show, he had a railroad boxcar dedicated to his booze and was known to actually send out for more when that was depleted.

Cody picked up his glass and took a long swallow. The hand that held the glass had a slight tremor, but Curly caught it. He peered over his drink and took a hard look at Cody. Suddenly it all made sense, the hitching step, the weaker voice, the sudden shift and repetition of conversation. Curly was seeing the beginnings of the decline of a giant.

That thought sickened Curly, who believed like the rest of America that Buffalo Bill Cody was ageless. He shifted uncomfortably in his seat. That got the attention of Cody, who, seeing Curly seated with drink in hand, got down to business.

"I'm here to buy a mine," he announced, "and I want to know if it might be part of the lost mine with the iron door."

Curly was a rather serious man, seldom smiling, and seldom surprised, but Cody shook him on this.

"You know, Bill" he began slowly, "most believe that mine is just a story. Never any proof the Spanish Jesuits found gold; never any evidence of a mine being shut up with an iron door. "

Cody's pacing indicated the level of his impatience. "I know Curly, but there's too much talk. You know what they say about smoke and fire. You know these mountains better than anyone 'cept Stratton. I want to know what you think, old Pard."

"Well I'll look, Bill, but don't get too excited about it."

Cody left the Mountain View a few days later after his meeting *with Ward. He had a show to prepare for the 1910 season, but he wasn't too happy about the coming season. For the first time he was not the sole owner of his show. Pawnee Bill had bought his debt markers and the Wild West Show was now part of the Pawnee Bill Great Far East Show.*

A year later on February 27, 1910, Cody was back at the Mountain View. This time, he brought Mrs. Cody with him. First thing Cody did was to check with Curly. He was anxious to hear what his scouting partner had to say about the mine with the iron door.

Curly was reluctant to report to Cody. "I've looked Bill, been looking for years, and really searched these hills for you, but can't find a thing." Curly paused, then cautiously continued. "I think there was a mine, but I think the earthquake of '87 buried it. 'Fore that, we could cut through the Cañada del Oro to Tucson, right where the "window" is now. I myself think that the mine is on the Tucson side of the Santa Catalina Mountains buried under all that rock. If you can get to a point in the mountains where you can look through the "window" and see San Xavier Mission, nine miles to the south, I think the mine is in that line."

Ever hopeful Cody pressed, "But the Southern Bell mines could be part of it."

Curly let out a huff. "Could be," he reluctantly agreed, "but we'll never know."

But Cody was desperate for money, and ever a dreamer — never a good combination. He looked at the Campo Bonito mine and decided he liked what he saw, or was told. A few months later, John Burgess and Cody posted a notice of a mining lode claim at Campo Bonito, in the Old Hat District, southwesterly from Oracle. Cody and Burgess were each listed as half owner. The claim included the Morning Star, Oro Fino and the Maudina mines.

In 1909, Cody was a national icon standing for adventure,

courage and toughness. He had become the template for the frontier plainsman. He was even more than that. To the world, he represented the ruggedness and mystic of the American West.

It could be said of Cody that not only did he define the American West, he designed it. The plays he appeared in, which eventually led to his Wild West shows, told of a west according to the melodramatic views of Cody, his writers and the demanding public. When he finally performed his plays out west, a crusty old-timer was heard to remark, "We may not have talked like that before but we sure do now."

Cody was a contradiction. He didn't swear, yet he surrounded himself with less than admirable characters with colorful vocabularies. He professed to be a God fearing man, yet he committed adultery and perpetuated lies about himself. He was a hard drinking man, and in later years, showed the signs of one on booze, yet he proclaimed he had given up liquor. He expounded on truth and his concern for the poor, yet he wrote glowing reports to his relatives and friends on mines that were not very productive and that he was trying to sell. He was in many ways a man of the times and yet uniquely himself.

Cody's real life was much like the penny novels that were written about him. Although these novels were fictional stories of the great plainsman, there was enough truth in them to make them very believable. For hundreds of people around the world, they represented a window into what was then shrouded in mystery, conjecture, and wild tales — the American West. Cody's stories introduced the reader to the Pony Express, scouting, buffalo hunts, and battles with the American Indians. The truth was stretched to pique the interest of the reader and later the viewer.

Cody was a rider for the Pony Express at the tender age of 14. On one assignment, he rode over three hundred miles when his relief had been killed. He proudly wore his "Buffalo Bill" nickname which he earned by killing over 4,200 buffalo to feed the railroad workers laying the lines. At the time, buffalo herds numbering millions covered the plains. The hunters never thought their killings would all but eliminate the beasts.

He was also a successful and daring scout for the Army, both in the Indian Wars and the Civil War, counting Sherman, Custer, and Sheridan among his satisfied customers. He won his Medal of Honor by scouting out the enemy and bringing a contingency of soldiers safely back to camp after an encounter with an Indian war party.

But for all his daring and courage, fame and fortune came from the unlikely source of show business. His first appearance on the stage was a fluke, brought about by a visit to a play written about him by Ned Buntline. Ned thought Cody could play himself better than some actor. He encouraged Cody to take the role in the plays. These dramas of the wild western life eventually gave birth to Cody's Wild West Show, which featured sharpshooters, bronco riders, real American Indians, and, later, a cadre of warriors from countries around the world, all playing out great battles and dramatic western encounters.

His Wild West Show brought him world recognition and millions of dollars. However, Cody's soft heart made him an easy touch for friends, as well as strangers and left him often without funds. He had a deeply-rooted need for riches and a strong false sense of financial responsibility toward his family and friends.

Cody fancied himself a businessman. Yet, his inability to sustain interest in anything as non-physical as managing a business, doomed most projects to failure. He was always on the lookout for a money-making venture. He was additionally hindered in his quest to make money by his basic lack of business sense and his inability to tell an honest man from a crooked one. He was brilliant in the ways of the outdoors, but lacked knowledge and intelligence for the more cerebral endeavors, like balance sheets.

His get-rich schemes included everything from manufacturing a coffee substitute to developing two towns. One of the towns was short-lived. It met its demise when the railroad took a bypass route. The other town met with more success and today, Cody, Wyoming is both commercial and historical.

As Cody aged, interest in the American West by an increasingly sophisticated world diminished. His income reflected this change in society. As his income decreased, the monetary demands of his family increased and he did nothing to rein in his generous ways.

His personal life was no less dramatic. Of his three daughters and one son, only Irma outlived her father. He was constantly in need of money, spent most of his life away from his family and lived in a failing marriage. In 1904, he filed for divorce from his wife Louisa Federici Cody, whom he married May 1, 1865. The divorce case did not go to court until 1905 when he return from Europe where he had been appearing with the Wild West Show.

He claimed incompatibility — "she's always nagging." She countered with infidelity. Neither proved their charges and the case ended with no divorce being granted and Lulu awarded court costs. After the divorce suit had ended, Lulu refused a reconciliation. In 1909, they finally achieved some sort of compromise when family members shut the two of them in a room and kept them there until peace was restored.

Although together again as man and wife, they were hardly a model couple. He didn't think she was much fun, and she believed he was very foolish and naïve to be parted from his money so easily. When he came to Arizona in 1910, Lulu came along. Lulu had no interest in mining. She spent her days sitting on the Mountain View porch, knitting away as she shared intimacies with Elizabeth Lambert Wood. Cody took himself off to Campo Bonito where he lived in a wooden and canvas tent, drank his booze, partied with Johnny Baker and friends and pitched gold dollars like pennies.

At 63, Cody found himself deep in debt, a show no longer his own, hotels going bankrupt, and his personal life in tatters. Life had conditioned him to believe that money was there, you just had to know where to look for it, then have the guts to grab it. Cody figured the place to look for money was in mining and he was going to grab it with his Oracle mines.

Mining was not a new venture for Cody. His first experience was when he was still in his teens. In between his scouting assignments he headed for gold country but soon returned a disappointed, but wiser man. But he never erased his lust for gold dust and was immediately interested when, in 1903, the self-styled "Captain" Burgess, a prospector, talked Cody into buying some mining property in Arizona.

Cody and his friend, Col. Daniel Burns Dyer, formed a mining partnership called The Cody-Dyer Arizona Mining and Milling Company. The mines consisted of more than twelve tunnels and the plan was for a small scale railroad to run between the tunnels and the mill. In a letter to his sister, Julia, in March, 1903, Cody claimed his property was worth millions and he would soon get some of the money when the mill was up and running. Until then, they planned on hauling ore by wagons to the smelter seven miles away. This operation depended on passable roads.

Cody had plans for his "millions." He told Julia he wanted to give his family all the money they needed and he planned to use the rest to help the poor, churches, and to do all sorts of charitable things.

His dream was never to be realized. While considerable ore was mined, it was never enough to produce a significant profit. Plagued by poor management, bad weather and undependable equipment, his mines never produced at the expected rate despite initial positive reports. The best of the properties barely made expenses.

This lack of success did not dim Cody's dreams of striking it rich. When Burgess came to him with an opportunity to add to his mine holdings with the Campo Bonito property, which included several mining claims, Cody jumped at the chance.

The timing was right for Burgess to sell his scheme. Cody was perilously close to bankruptcy. One night over drinks at the Union Club in New York, Cody and Dyer decided to add the Campo Bonito claims to their Arizona mining properties.

Cody believed his finances were about to change. He had reason to be excited. A recent engineering report told of the possibility of great wealth from this mining property. Cody never thought to seek a second report, or to doubt the veracity of the reporting engineer. Cody never doubted any man's word, which proved to be unfortunate in this case as the report was based more on fiction than fact.

By the end of 1910, Cody's finances were a disaster. He had hopes of retirement but his hotel properties and his ranches were losing money. He was now 64, plagued with health problems and deeply concerned about his finances.

Preoccupied, he presented prime-picking for the unscrupulous mining men he trusted and became dependent upon: R. Brady with the Southern Belle property, J.D. Burgess and Campo Bonito, and his mine managers, the Getchells. He also found at the end, that his good friend and partner, Col. Dyer, was less than honest with him.

L.W. Getchell and his son Noble were hired to manage the

Campo Bonito mining property. That began what was almost a one-way correspondence between Cody and Getchell with Cody constantly demanding, then pleading, and then begging for mining reports.

In June of 1910 Cody wrote to Getchell chastising him for not remembering his show route and sending reports to the wrong places. He demanded Getchell let him know how much scheelite was above the 153 foot level and how the vein was pitching. He complained about expenses.

Just a few months later, Cody wrote Getchell that Major Lillie (also known as Pawnee Bill) was interested in the mine. Lillie had over $500,000 in cash that he could invest but wanted to see the ore mines for himself. He was arriving in Tucson in October and Cody ordered his manager to take Lillie around and give him a show.

For the first time, Cody began to have doubts about Campo Bonito. Lillie must of had these same doubts, for he never invested in the mine.

The mine was taking much of Cody's cash and so far, there had been no payback. The mill construction was two months behind schedule. Cody had told his manager to order everything that was needed to build the mill and have it on hand. Apparently, this was never done. That same month Cody made the final payment of $1,025 on the mine property. He was also able to send Getchell $500 for expenses, but admonished him to spend the money wisely, as the show had not produced the amount of money expected and the season was just about over. He wrote, "Bonito must start producing or it will be left with only a watchman. If it is not on a paying basis by the time I get there, we will let everyone go."

By the end of 1910, Cody had invested $70,000 for operations and some development. All this did little to produce ore.

Buffalo Bill and his wife Lulu spent the beginning months of 1911 in Oracle. He arrived from Tucson in a Packard touring car driven by Herbert Bowyer, Curly's ranch foreman. Curly knew as soon as he saw his old partner that he was not well. His gait was hesitant; his grip not too firm. Arthritis and a painful prostate were slowing down the old scout. His high-living lifestyle was hastening the process.

Cody had built an elaborate hideout at Campo Bonito called High Jinks. The mine shaft there had originally been opened by Johnny Baker for the Cody-Dyer Arizona Mining and Milling Company. Cody stayed there, partying, and enjoying his mine. Lulu stayed at the Mountain View.

That year, Cody began what proved to be a disastrous show season. Poor health was beginning to slow him down. He had problems sorting fact from fiction, confusing much of what was fabricated about him with reality. He began missing performances when he couldn't mount up.

June of that year proved to be a nightmare month. Cody caught the grippe but ill as he was, he still had to perform. Then, leaving Boston, the show train had a wreck. Livestock was scattered over the countryside. Cowboys had to roundup horses, buffalo and cattle from the countryside in the pouring rain. Some were never found. The wreck cost the company $10,000 in damages. That, combined with the losses at the gate, meant Cody had problems meeting his mine payroll.

By this time, the partners had over 45 claims and some scheelite was being mined. But friends thought the Getschells were robbing Cody. That summer, Cody received a report on the Campo Bonito mine from James Russell a mining engineer. Russell wrote to Cody that he was being shamefully imposed upon and should pay attention to the last part of the Southern Belle property.

Cody had taken a lease on the Southern Belle from R. Brady, but Brady was leasing the land from Mrs. Coddington. As payment on the property Brady had received a note from Cody for $14,000. Nobel Getschell was supposed to receive half of that from Brady. But Brady took off for Kansas City, signed the note over, pocketed the money and went his way. At the end of the year, Cody still had not received the deed from Mrs. Coddington who had inherited the land from Ed Fellows.

Talk at the Mountain View was that the Getschell's were paying a pittance for mines adjacent to Campo Bonito and charging Cody ten times the amount.

Cody decided to send his trusted foster son, Lewis Johnny Baker, to investigate the management of the mines. Baker found a number of discrepancies including a padded payroll. Thirty six names were listed but only four men were working.

Cody fired a letter off to Getchell saying he had nearly bankrupted himself believing what he had been told. However, he still spoke of his confidence in the Getchells. He wanted to know if he should go ahead or quit, stating he was nearly crazy from lack of information.

By fall, Cody's frustration had reached a new level. Getschell continually demanded money with promises of high price ore being attainable if they had the right equipment, or more time or more workers.

More mine problems arrived in the form of three weeks of rain and cloud bursts which washed out bridges and wagon roads. This delayed the arrival of equipment for the railroad and the mill.

Cody's next letter to Getschell stated his frustration. He accused Getschell of not writing and explaining anything. He mentioned Dyer's patience was exhausted and that he himself was sick and discouraged. He and Dyer believed Getschell and his son were holding the mill back. Mrs. Coddington had not sent the deed and Cody was not going to pay any more money until she deposited the deed. He insisted it be recorded in Pinal County immediately.

Cody was facing serious financial problems and his poor health exacerbated his plight. Money was not available but the demands for it were. Cody's sister, May Decker, and her husband were managing the Irma Hotel, Cody's two other hotels and the Trail's End Ranch. May's constant whining and demands for money were bleeding Cody dry. Whatever was left went into the mines. Now Cody's notes were due. When Harry Tammen offered Cody a $20,000 loan, Cody saw it as his salvation and quickly signed the papers.

Perhaps Cody was not solvent, but he was still the nation's hero. Newspaper headlines across the country announced William F. Cody's intentions to become the new state of Arizona's first senator. Cody was agreeable if Arizona became a state that year (1911). Arizona, however, was not granted statehood until February 14, 1912, thus missing out on having a senator known nationally and internationally before serving.

On his trip to the mine that year, Cody visited the home of Burgess and his daughter Maud. While there, he noticed a wagon pull up and cases of canned goods being unloaded. Something did not strike him as right, but before he could investigate Maude insisted he relax and have another drink.

That spark of suspicion did not go away. He wondered if the canned goods were part of a company store order that had been sidetracked.

Cody did nothing about his suspicions at that time, but by the beginning of 1912, Cody and Dyer had had enough with the lack of production at their mines, and reports that promised much but produced excuses. Johnny Baker again made a quick trip out to the Oracle mines. This time he found outsiders were stealing ore from the mine. Some $3,000 worth of gold was missing. Johnny started a policy of searching the miners as they left the tunnels.

That was enough to convince Cody and Dyer that there was some underhanded business going on. They contacted Dyer's nephew, Ernest Julius (E.J.) Ewing, who was a mining engineer, and instructed him to go out and have a look around Campo Bonito.

Cody sent Johnny Baker to Oracle to meet with Ewing. The two meet in Baker's room at the Mountain View Hotel. They decided the best strategy was for them not to acknowledge knowing each other when they met at the mine. Ewing was to sign on as a mine worker.

Ewing's investigations at the mine produced some startling discoveries for the trusting Cody. Arriving at the mine site, he discovered a Mexican pouring scheelite concentrates into the feed stream. This succeeded in widening the concentration band by almost a foot. While the long tunnel of the mine ran for a considerable length, it was only 25 feet below the earth's surface.

Ewing also found evidence that the Getschells were receiving kickbacks. Cody threatened them with arrest and prosecution. They finally agreed to give up their mining stock and return some of the company's money to Cody. In return, Cody decided not to prosecute.

Cody still believed the mine had all the signs of being the mother lode of all mines. He felt it was the best answer to his financial dilemma.

Ewing's initial reports were not promising. He informed the owners that there was no indication on Campo Bonito or Southern Belle that there would be any immediate profits. It was time for them to make a decision. Either they sell the controlling interest in the mines to interested New York parties and use their profits for legitimate prospecting and debt payments, or they prove the property by development work as soon as possible, so that they could hold on to it. In order to maintain ownership to a claim, owners had to "prove" their mines by completing and recording a $100 worth of work a year.

In March, Cody sent Ewing $500 and a request for information on the Maudina mine and Campo Bonito. Ewing warned Cody that the claims were open to being jumped because unassessed work was not up to date.

Cody was still interested in selling and, toward that goal, advised Ewing on June fourth not to mine a sheelite vein but to leave it in place so the mine would show to the best advantage. Ten days later, he ordered the prove work to be done on the mines.

Things became financially difficult for Ewing during the summer because he had not received the money Cody had arranged to be sent. Ewing closed down the High Jinks. Disgruntled workers started rumors that the company was bankrupt.

To raise much needed operating capital, Cody sent his foster son, Johnny Baker, to London to sell the company's mining stock. Cody even contacted his friend, Thomas A. Edison, hoping for some funding for the mine. Already half a million dollars had been dropped into it.

Now, a frantic Cody approached Anheuser Busch with an offer to sell his Hotel Irma in Cody, Wyoming and both of his Yellowstone Hotels as a package. He was willing to give him a big game hunt and stay at the hotels as a host until the end of the hunting season. Nothing ever came of Cody's proposition.

Ewing was still showing the property to interested investors. He was escorting a Mr. Helm around the mine, telling him what a fine, trouble-free camp it was, when trouble hit. Two of the former workers, Ramires and Torres, had an on-going feud. That day, they went gunning for each other. Ramires got off the first shot and put a hole the size of a silver dollar in Torres' back. Drenched in blood, a weak Torres insisted he would pull through. Ewing doubted he'd live to see Oracle.

Ewing proposed mining be suspended and some basic work be performed. Cody requested they run some ore from the Cody Tunnel. By fall, Ewing pronounced the mill to be in good shape.

Before Cody could enjoy this information, he was told Burgess wanted his payment of $2,500 which was due him when the claims were patented. However, there was some concerns as Burgess sold more claims than the survey showed.

Ewing had a new strike in September. Cody was delighted and demanded specific information. He stated it was now up to Ewing, for he was ideally placed to get intelligent information on how and what to ship from the mine.

Ewing suggested they take out the "pay dirt" and run it through the mill to show a profit. He believed they could run the mill for ten hours and asked if Cody wanted to get an immediate return or show the mine at its best advantage.

Cody, ever the big dreamer, wanted both. He told Ewing to run through a ton of concentrate so that a company could bid on it. Then he instructed Ewing to expose two or three good looking places so they could be seen by potential buyers.

Cody sent Ewing instructions on selling the concentrates, telling him to get bids from Atkins and Dross. He wanted Ewing to keep good records, weigh the concentrates and post them in the mill book to impress potential investors.

Cody wrote enthusiastic letters to his cousin Frank Cody in Canada bragging about how promising the mines were and encouraging him to sell stock to his friends and connections.

By the end of the year, Cody faced the truth. His Oracle mines could not produce enough to finance his retirement and his huge debts made it impossible for him to quit show business. To cut his expenses the Cody-Dyer company decided to let their option lapse on the Southern Belle mine group. Although they had found scheelite in course particles there, the operation costs could not be covered. Years later, Elizabeth Lambert Wood was to make her fortune on this claim.

Cody's show business career did not fare any better in 1912 than his mining operation. The box office lost money as bad weather forced show cancellations. Heartsick over his problems, Cody and Lulu went to the Mountain View and Campo Bonito for Christmas. There, against a background of mountains and his mine, Cody found balm for his soul by playing Santa Claus for the children of Oracle. He gave them a treat they never forgot.

Santa appeared to the children and spoke in the strange tongue of the Sioux. In front of a huge decorated tree, Cody, in a red suit with his white flowing beard and long locks, looked every bit the part. He handed out dolls for the girls, tops for the boys and candy for all.

It was a festive occasion made even more special with music and dancing. However, some said the highlight of the day was the fat man's race between J. Frank Cody, the scout's cousin, and Professor William Sweeney, the longtime leader of the Buffalo Bill Wild West band. Cousin Frank Cody won the race by fifty yards, thus holding up the family name.

Show profits in 1913 were even less than past years. Poor

weather contributed to the small audiences. Also, this was the third year that Cody appeared in his "farewell show." People were losing interest and the gate lost money for 100 successive days.

It all came to a dramatic end in July of that year. In Denver, pressured by Tammen, who held the paper on Cody's loan, the sheriff foreclosed on the Wild West Show. Everything was confiscated and sold at auction leaving Cody with no hope to mount another show.

In desperation, Cody applied to the adjutant general of the Army for pay he thought was due as a Medal of Honor holder. But Army Regulations in 1913 stated that only members of the Army could receive the medal and the payment. Cody was a civilian when he had been awarded. Now his name was stricken from the list of holders.

Cody realized he had to start over. In a creative and far thinking move, he made plans to film the Indian War battles. The Army supplied 600 troopers. General Mills and other Indian War veterans volunteered to reenact the events. The cast included Indians who had been in the Wild West Show along with members of the Pine Ridge Reservation. When finished, the movie consisted of eight reels. Cody's son-in-law was tasked with promoting the films but he could find few takers.

Cody was concerned about the possibility of losing his mining properties to the government. He instructed Ewing to be sure and pay all taxes, especially on the Southern Belle. He also wanted to know how much more assessment work had to be done on Campo Bonito. Apparently the Canadians were ready to talk terms.

Mr. Bourne, the Pinal Tax Collector, kept the books open for Ewing so that the taxes would not go on the delinquent list. But bad luck still followed Cody. At the end of the year the Southern Belle house caught fire and could not be saved.

Ewing had to complete work on the Maudina mine, the three claims in the Flag group, and the two claims in the Dane group by the end of the year. He didn't think the required work could be finished in time and had decided to bluff it. His bluff succeeded. Records show an Affidavit of Labor Performed and Improvements Made was filed by Ewing on the last day of the year. It included the Alexandra, Dane, Gideon, Emily and Pinchot mines.

Cody did get some good news from his Oracle mines. Ewing had found what he believed to be a pure gold vein, about five feet in length. Samples assessed out from a trace to $45. He wrote Cody that the ore showed up well and was full of minerals. The vein was big and strong which meant there was a good chance of finding some other valuable ore.

On the lighter side, Ewing informed Cody that Fred had planted rose bushes, ivy, flowers, wheat, lettuce and radishes around his teepee at High Jinks.

The seizure and closing of Buffalo Bill's Wild West Show now left Cody at the mercy of Harry Tammen. Tammen's loan to Cody, in 1911, stipulated he could demand Cody's professional services. He now did just that for his Sell-Floto circus.

Cody started his tour with the Sell-Floto Circus at the beginning of 1914. The circus made appearances along the west coast and in Canada. Cody was required to introduce the show from the saddle and make himself available on the circus grounds. For this, he would receive one hundred dollars a day and 40% of receipts over $3,000; far less than his earnings from the Wild West Show. As tired and as sick as he was, this routine became physically and emotionally painful.

The season ended in Texas in mid-October. Cody then negotiated his next year's contract, unfortunately to his disadvantage. The base for his percentage was raised from $3,000 to $3,100. He would still get his $100 a day.

Cody could no longer afford his mines. On Ewing's advice, he discharged miners and decided to work Campo Bonito on a smaller scale. He kept the Maudina and Morning Star mines working as they were the only ones producing, but profits were low. Cody proposed the Cody-Dyer Company invest in start up operations, as the mill was in good condition. He did not have the money to personally fund the operation on his own and turned to his partner Dyer. But Dyer was ill and died that year, leaving his estate in tangles. Dyer's heirs were not interested in investing in mining.

The mines next to Cody's, owned by Charlie Brajevich, were available. The asking price was a minimum of $20,000. Cody was appalled at this price tag on the Brajevich's mines and wrote to Mrs. Coddington telling her, that when he bought the Southern Belle, he believed the Brajevich claims were part of it. He was willing to fight this issue and believed Mrs. Coddington did not want a lawsuit.

By the middle of the year, Cody had not received any money from his movies and wanted to sell the whole mining operation. Ewing continued to manage the mining business, and under his supervision the finances and operations were in good shape. He informed Cody that with additional funding, they could work on the Belle veins without interference.

In 1914, Johnny Baker was in London trying to raise British capital for the Oracle mines. Things looked promising for Cody. He wrote Ewing that he had two buyers for his mine and tungsten was five times higher than its previous market value. In a letter to his cousin Frank, Cody announced a new scheelite strike.

Johnny's trip produced no revenue, however Burgess

found an investor that was willing to take an option on the Southern Belle. The price was to be $125,000 with the following arrangements: payments of $12,500 every six months for two years with the balance due at the end of the two years. Burgess also offered to find a purchaser for the Bonito claims and, if within two months none could be found, he would take an option on them for the same terms offered on the Southern Belle property.

Cody started 1915 in a hopeful frame of mine. He told Ewing that some Denver people were serious and wanted the mines. The Denver deal fell through when their mining engineer was delayed in Mexico and couldn't get to the Oracle mines for his evaluation.

Cody celebrated his 69th birthday in Cody, Wyoming. The town gave him a magnificent party at the Irma Hotel. He started the show season fit and rested. Again, nature conspired with the elements to give Cody a horrible season. The show had only four days of sunshine in the first six weeks of the tour. At Fort Madison the show was flooded out. The tents were pitched near a swamp and as the turbulent waters rose, Cody and five of his men worked to rescue the women and children.

Cody was upset with the conditions of the show and the unscrupulous way Tammen, owner of the Sell-Floto Circus, did business. He was angry enough to kill and Tammen knew it. Cody wanted out. Tammen arranged a meeting with Cody after he had been assured Cody would do him no bodily harm. He got Cody to agree to stay with the show until the end of the season. Tammen promised not to dock Cody's pay for his debt and threatened a $100,000 lawsuit if Cody broke the contract.

That year Cody, gave 366 performances and traveled almost 17,000 miles with the show. At the end of the season he paid $5,000 to buy back his name. He was finally finished with the man he claimed broke his heart.

Cody still had great hopes for his Oracle mine but needed money to work the mine properly. He was able to generate some income by writing a series of autobiographical articles entitled *The Great West That Was: Buffalo Bill's Life Story* for William Randolph Hearst's international magazine. He also leased 1500 acres of oil land in Wyoming and started the Buffalo Bill Oil and Gas Company.

In 1916, American was preparing for war. A neutral nation was dealing with the sinking of the Lusitania. Seeing a business opportunity, Cody decided to create a show called "A Pageant of Preparedness" that could be performed along with his Wild West Show. He was able to interest the Army and was promised he could use soldiers on leave and artillery pieces. Unable to fund his own show, he joined the 101 Ranch Wild West Show.

Cody's experiences of working for another show were much different this time around. He was paid $100 a day and one third of the profits over a daily take of $2,750. However, his debts were such that many times he had to draw an advance to pay his bills.

His mining luck seem to be changing for the good. In the summer of 1916, he wrote that Campo Bonito was working nearly 50 men and running night and day. But again his good fortune was short-lived; tungsten prices slumped. Ewing advised Cody to cut back to a smaller operation.

That year, E.J. Ewing became Secretary-Treasurer of the Gorman & Sebring Company. Out at the mine site Ewing and an old prospector found "wolfram" (a tungsten ore) and traced it to its source. On a ridge below the Oro Fino mine, they found sheelite. With just the two of them working, they located five or six claims and sold them for $5,000 each. Ewing took a lease out on the Maudina Mine and had the mill running by February of that year.

A royalty of 25% was paid to Cody on the work done. With this, all of the Cody's indebtedness was erased except for a $10,000 obligation to one Barney Link for work done by the New York Bill Posting Company. This debt had been incurred by Cody's Wild West Show.

Johnny Baker was back at the Oracle mines in November, 1916. There, he discovered Max Junghandle, a mining expert who represented a German syndicate, checking out the mines. Mr. Junghandle was so impressed with what he found, he was ready to make an offer for the Cody-Dyer mines. Again Cody was sure he had found a buyer for his mines and his spirits soared. But the deal was never completed.

At seventy, Cody's health was declining. He was exhausted most of the time and suffering from uremic poisoning, which was affecting his kidneys and heart. He was pale, gaunt and hollowed eyed. By the end of the tour, Johnny Baker had to help him into the saddle. In his last days, he could not even sit his horse. He kept up a good front with his family, writing to his sister Julia that he was in good health and making money.

The show he was appearing in closed in Virginia in November. Cody went to Denver to visit his sister May, then had plans to travel on to his Trails End Ranch in Wyoming. While visiting May, he caught a cold, and his run down condition could do little to fight it off. Complications resulted from a weakened heart and stomach trouble. His wife and daughter were sent for, but Cody rallied.

Cody and his physician Dr. East traveled to Glenwood Springs in January, 1917, for the curative waters. Just before leaving the Springs, Dr. East released a statement on Cody's health, announcing the Old Scout was suffering from a nervous collapse, his memory was virtually gone, and he did not have long to live. The doctor also blamed part of Cody's condition on the full moon.

Cody returned to his sister May's house in Denver. There with Lulu, his daughter, his sister Julia and his son-in-law Garlow by his side he died on January 10, 1917.

He never saw the riches from his Oracle mines. The mines produced their first real profit in 1918. Over the years, several people made their fortune with the Southern Belle mines. But, none was William Frederick Cody.

The rapid decline of Cody's health was due to his excessive drinking throughout his life. His emotional unhappiness came from his worries over his large debts, all incurred to keep up his expansive lifestyle, and his unrealistic business dreams. He continually chased his rainbow only to find, not a pot of gold at the end, but a big deep hole called Campo Bonito.

After Cody's death, the Link estate claimed the mines and E.J. Ewing managed them for that estate from 1918 until September 1943.

The High Jinks land was bought by the High J. Gold Mining Company, Incorporated. When they failed to pay the taxes, Captain Lewis Claude Way bought the property. Captain Way was in the Forest Service and spent most of his working career in the Oracle/Mt. Lemmon area. Between 1922 and 1927, Captain Lewis Claude Way built the Casa High Jinks. His wife Marie was the sister of Oliva, the widow of Johnny Baker, Cody's beloved foster son.

Until her death, Oliva Baker spent part of the year at High Jinks. She opened the High Jinks originally as a mini-museum proudly showing Cody's possessions, including his Medal of Honor. High Jinks is now privately owned, but is listed on the National Register of Historic Places.

The house is one with the land. Made of stone and wood construction, it rises toward the sky with a powerful thrust, and is topped by a bank of windows that look out over the Galiuro and the Catalina Mountains. The wind here is strong and sometimes, as it flows over the hills and canyons, you can hear the clink, clink, clink of pitched coins. If you are lucky, and listen carefully, you might hear the booming voice of a showman in the thunder that rolls off the mountains.

ALEXANDER MCKAY
1841 - 1910

The McKay Ranch House with the ranch cook in front   Oracle Historical Society

FROM THE MOUNTAIN VIEW HOTEL REGISTER,
APRIL 19, 1910

CHAPTER 8:
THE PROSPECTOR

It rained last night. This morning the sky was a clear, clean blue on which a line of fluffy clouds drifted. It was as if Mother Nature had hung her white wash above the Catalina Mountains to dry. Alex McKay stood on the Mountain View porch, bracing his wiry body and deeply inhaling the strong scent of creosote. How different this air was from the highlands of Scotland. Although it was fifty-four years since he left his birthplace in Perth, he could still remember the heather hills and the cold winds that swept down the craggy mountains. He was fifteen when he left to seek adventure. He finally found it in the color of gold in these Arizona Mountains.

Stepping over to one of the rockers, McKay sat down and viewed the rolling land before him. Scattered over these Santa Catalina foothills were at least a dozen houses and ranches. From where he sat, he could only see a few. Across the road was Neal's gable cottage and around the hotel were horse corrals, the outdoor dance floor, and high grassy hills. In the distance, he could make out the mountains that stretched to Redington and Mammoth.

He believed he had walked every trail, poked in every crevice, and bore holes in every ridge of these mountains. That was in his prospecting days. Now he tried to take life easy. But an easy life wasn't easy for him. He could feel the restlessness welling up in him, enough to choke him. That's why he hitched a ride up here with Buffalo Bill's crew.

He had spotted them at the Tucson train station the day before. They were a colorful lot, and noisy to boot. When he heard they were headed for Neal's Mountain View Hotel, he decided to tag along. It had been a long time since he surveyed these hills.

The first time had been about '78. McKay settled his bones into the rocker and thought about his first trip to the Santa Catalina Mountains. He had met Albert Weldon in Tucson, and one thing led to another. Weldon had invited him up to these mountains to see the mine he and Jimmie Lee had located. There was nothing in the area then but Indian and game trails.

The sound of the front door banging open brought McKay out of his reverie. The three members of Cody's Wild West Show jostled their way out the door with good humor. Henry Finn, Mayor Burke and Fred Weidermanning had come to Oracle with Buffalo Bill to enjoy a brief vacation while Cody tended to his mines. Cody's troop enjoyed coming to the Mountain View. Annie Neal, the proprietress, managed to keep her Wild West guests happy with, picnics, dances, rodeos and shooting competitions.

The three showman were staying at the Mountain View; Cody, however, preferred staying at his Campo Bonito mine, mostly to get away from the watchful eye of Mrs. Cody who enjoyed the more civilized lifestyle of the Mountain View.

Cody had a great interest in mines. He believed he could strike it rich; and he believed he would do it in the Santa Catalinas, but so far his mines in the Santa Catalina Mountains were costing him more than he was hauling out.

One of the reasons McKay had decided to come up to the Mountain View was for the excitement the show people always generated. And, McKay was always looking for excitement! His life was getting dull. He wasn't working a claim, and the lifestyle of a landowner in Tucson really didn't suit him. His paramour, Rosalia, did that much better. He was bored with sheep ranching and was considering selling his ranch to Charles Bayless. It was time he headed out and did some prospecting. That was another good reason to come back to the Santa Catalina Mountains. His first claims were located not far from the Mountain View Hotel. He was a part of this land.

Alexander McKay was a wandering bird. When he first came west he spent ten years in California shearing sheep. When that work ended, he headed for Flagstaff. He had heard about sheep shearing work there. McKay made it as far as Yuma — only to find the river was low due to the dry spell and the northbound boat, the Ehrenbeurg, was high and dry.

Yuma was not the place to be in 1877. A smallpox epidemic was ravaging the town. There weren't many places to go from there. McKay's choices were back to California or on to Tucson. He chose Tucson. It took him a week to get out of town and by the time he arrived in Tucson, his money was gone. Someone directed him to W. C. Davis who was known to help down-and-out miners. Davis had a tin shop on the southeast corner of Main and Congress. But Davis couldn't help him and advised McKay to head for Tombstone.

By this time, McKay had had enough of Arizona. The weather was beginning to heat up so he decided to head for Colorado. Heading north, he found work at the Heintzelman mine and got a mining education along with it. His days, and some of his nights, were spent draining water out of mine shafts and setting timbers. Most of the work was at the 250-foot level where three veins of four-inch native wire silver were located.

Four months in the mine were enough to convince McKay to go prospecting on his own. He headed back to Tucson where he ran into Albert Weldon who asked him to come up to Oracle Camp and see his mine. He outfitted a couple of mules and headed for the mountains northwest of Tucson. Oracle Camp was situated on a ridge. Nearby was a good size spring with sparkling clean water. He pitched his fly tent, set up camp and went prospecting.

Living in that fly tent turned out to be dangerous. Wild animals such as bear, coyote, rattlesnakes and deer used the nearby trails to the springs. And that was just the wildlife dangers. This was also Apache land. The evidence of their presence was all around the mountains in those days. Sometimes, you could hear the gunfire of the Indian and soldier encounters. The trails in the Cañada del Oro were littered with bullet casings from these skirmishes.

In one of these meetings, the Apaches massacred a small troop of soldiers who were on their way from Ft. Lowell in Tucson to Camp Grant north of Oracle. He remembered hearing the gun shots. By the time he got there, it was all over. Looking around at the scene, he discovered an abandoned Apache child wandering in the brush. She was a tiny mite, just able to walk. McKay carried her up to Jimmie Lee and his family who were living in the hills. They took her in and raised her as their own. She grew up to be quite a lovely woman and eventually married Antonio Feliz.

Antonio Feliz was an interesting character. He knew just about everything there was to know about raising cattle. He taught George S. Wilson the cattle business and worked as the main vaquero on Wilson's Linda Vista Ranch.

Tony was well liked and quite respected in around the village of Oracle. When Hollywood came to the town to film Harold Bell Wright's *The Mine with the Iron Door*, Tony was given a bit part. The day of the preview in Tucson, Wilson loaned Tony his truck to transport his whole family to see the movie. Tony was so exited he began celebrating a little early. He got so drunk in town he never saw the film. His family on the other hand enjoyed it very much and frequently talked about it, to Tony's chagrin.

Apache renegade bands were all over the area. You never knew when you might meet one. The situation was so dangerous, that news had spread as far as New York City. An August 1882 edition featured a front page article on the Indian war party led by Eskiminzin. McKay tried to avoid the Indian bands, but sometimes that was hard, like that day he was baking bread in his Dutch oven outside his tent.

It was the whistle that got his immediate attention. As far

as he knew there was no one else around. Startled, he looked up to find an Indian heading right for him. "Me George," the Indian announced. "Me Eskiminzin's man. More come. Eskiminzin come."

Right after that speech, a small band of Indian men, women and children topped the rise. Tied to their pack were two hindquarters of venison. Eskiminzin's man George asked for some flour. Now McKay knew they were going to get that flour whether he agreed or not. He figured a little trading might be in order.

The Indians got their flour, and he ended up with a quarter of venison. The trading done, McKay figured the Indian band would move on and was surprised and down-right concerned when they set up camp next to his tent. With this he really got nervous and spent a fitful night with half an eye on them. The next morning, McKay decided not to go prospecting instead he sat up on the hill, watching the camp. Much to his relief the Indians left his camp alone and soon moved on.

Eskiminzin and his small band lived and roamed the Galiuro Mountains, a range north of the Santa Catalinas. He camped at the former Camp Grant site, where an old stage stop used to be at the confluence of the San Pedro and the Aravaipa Rivers. That's where Eskiminzin was when the Papagos and the white men from Tucson slaughtered most of his tribe. He was half-crazy after that.

McKay remember hearing a story about Eskiminzin's visits to the Pierson cattle ranch, near Oracle village. What was left of Eskiminzin's tribe came to that ranch to gather acorns.

Mr. Pierson had a brier pipe shaped like a bull's head with horns. The tongue and eyes were rubies, the horns ivory. Old Eskiminzin badly wanted that pipe. He offered to trade his youngest wife for that pipe, but Pierson wouldn't let it go, so the Indian decided to ambush Pierson on the trail one night.

Eskiminzin hid on a rock ledge with the sun behind him and as Pierson rode by the old Indian jumped. But the wily pioneer knew he was there, and he ducked. The old Indian flew over Pierson, then, quickly jumped up shouting "Heep good Indian, heep good Indian." After his pronouncement Eskiminzin took off running for the hills, not waiting to see if he was believed.

The first Christmas McKay spent in Oracle was lucky for him. That was the day he located his first Santa Catalina mine and named it the Christmas mine. The next week he located the New Year mine. Over the following years, he would located the Wadsworth mine and then the Crocker and the Baboquivari mines.

It was the lure of gold that kept McKay in the Oracle area. However, his prospecting blood needed more than the search for gold. He was a man who enjoyed the good life. And the good life was drinking, gambling and having fun. Frequent trips to Tucson supplied all these things. One of his favorite fun companions in Tucson was George O. Hand. On one excursion Hand, McKay, and a man called Marsh managed to get pretty "full," as Hand put it. Marsh tried to take care of McKay, but Hand was only able to put himself to bed.

Not two months after that episode, McKay was back in town but this time it was to pay off his debts. He had money from the first installment on his mines. He spent the day looking for men he owed. He didn't have any problems finding them once word got out that he had money.

In June, McKay came into Tucson from his mine and was given $100 for some ore. The money disappeared fast playing "Monte,". Four days later, he was still in town and on a big drunk. Not being quite sober he lost his pocketbook in a privy and had to borrow a lantern from Hand to fish it out. It was worth fishing for; it contained $5000 in greenbacks and some St. Louis bank drafts.

McKay did a few other things in Tucson besides drink and gamble. One Christmas, he bought presents for some children in Tucson and made Hand go with him to deliver the gifts. Another time he insisted that Hand accompany him to meet a woman. Hand never said much about that meeting but he did write in his diary an oblique underlined statement: "Saw her."

About this time McKay was fed up with living in a tent. Ever mindful of the proximity of the Apaches in Oracle, he decided it was time to build a safe place to live. He began construction on a one-room adobe he would share with Weldon, his prospecting partner. Making their own bricks from the dirt on the ridge in back of them, they were able to complete the small dwelling in 1879.

That meager building was the start of Oracle village. Soon after the adobe was completed, W.H. Reed, a Tucson carpenter, built a house about a quarter mile down the road from McKay, where the Mountain View Hotel now stands. That house was also a tavern and found plenty of business with the prospectors in the area. Eventually Reed turned the property over to J.C. Waterman and went up to the top of the Santa Catalina Mountain range to establish a logging camp with Ira Carter.

Reed and Carter were homesteading 160 acres up there, when Sara Lemmon, her husband and E.O. Stratton, climbed to the top of the Santa Catalina Mountains. The Lemmons were botanists and had been trying to reach the summit from the southeastern end of the mountains. They were discouraged by their failure and were about to give up when McKay met them in Tucson on one of his frequent trips there. They were determined and he knew just the person to get them up that mountain.

Emerson O. Stratton had been working these mountains for a few years. He did some prospecting, some ranching, and lots of traveling around. McKay brought the Lemmons back to Oracle with him and introduced them to E.O. Stratton who outfitted them with two mules, one for riding and one for packing. That was a sight to see. There was Stratton leading the pack mule, walking behind him was Miss Sara, and bringing up the rear was her husband riding the other mule.

Sara was the first white woman known to reach the summit. In her honor, Stratton named the Mountain after her. He called it Mount Lemmon. Mount Sara probably didn't sound imposing enough. To honor the occasion they all carved their names and the year on a tree trunk.

Oracle just kept growing. By the turn of the century, it had two hotels, a store, and over a dozen houses tucked haphazardly over the hills. An older hotel called the Acadia Ranch was about a quarter mile down the road from the newer Mountain View Hotel, and the huge elegant Steward house sat imposingly on the road into the town. The Estill store was in between, and their house was on a hill above the store.

Two factors gave the area a boost. One was the discovery by a German doctor of the benefits of the local climate on consumptives. It all started when the Dodges came up from Tucson for Mrs. Dodge's health about 1880. The Oracle air was so good for her that she encouraged her friends to visit. So many of them visited, that the Dodge's turned their Acadia Ranch into a hotel for people with lung problems. The German doctor was one of their guests. He was so impressed with the effects of the clean air and fresh water on consumptives, that he published an article in a medical journal. That article resulted in an international reputation for Oracle.

The other factor was the discovery of gold. Isaac Loraine and Bill Henecke were working a claim they called the American Flag in Peppersauce Canyon, about five miles up the road on the way to Mount Lemmon. They found some good ore of silver and lead in the mine, but Mrs. Loraine had the biggest find. Out walking one day, she stopped to rest near the big white ledge behind the American Flag mine. Absentmindedly she broke off a piece of the ledge. It contained free course heavy gold. She sold the claim and the company put up the first mill in the area.

In its mining heyday, the American Flag employed over forty people and was the area's first post office. Eventually the vein played out and the Loraines turned the American Flag into a cattle ranch.

In 1880, McKay decided to leave the Arizona Territory with Roark, one of his partners, and go prospecting in Mexico. They reached the Burro Mountains but were stopped there by soldiers. The Apache Victoria was on the warpath, and Mexican government soldiers were everywhere. One morning as McKay rode up to the top of a high pass, he spotted a band of Indians coming up the other side. He was sure it was all over for Roark and himself. Not having much of a choice, they continued on.

Down the other side of the pass, they met a small troop of soldiers who told him they were looking for Indians. "My God, man," McKay blurted out, " I just passed about a dozen on the other side of the hill." The soldiers thought that was quite funny and said that they were Indian scouts. They explained that the friendly Indians wore white rags around their heads and the ones on the warpath wore red. McKay often wondered how many Indians had both headbands.

Having trouble telling the good Indians from the bad, and lacking success in his prospecting, McKay decided to return to Oracle from Mexico in 1882. By this time his Arizona mines were not very productive. He was still working the Christmas mine but it was hit and miss. McKay decided to speed up things and asked a friend to put a shot into the hanging wall of the mine. This he believed would release and expose the vein. Following McKay's orders, the man shot into the wall, but the shot hit an underground stream and flooded the mine. That was the end of the Christmas Mine.

With few prospects McKay decided to turn his holdings into a ranch. He laid over four miles of pipe, built a rock corral and a house. Next, he and W.C. Davis acquired about 400 sheep. Later they bought 6,500 more sheep from Sanford. But McKay hadn't totally given up on prospecting and, in 1883, he turned the sheep ranch over to the care of Bruce Maxwell and headed for the Quijotoa Mountains, southwest of Tucson. It was here that he made his most lucrative finds with the Peer, Peerless and Crocker mines. It wasn't all expertise that made McKay a successful prospector; some of it was dumb luck.

On a sizzling August day, he and a couple of his partners were out prospecting when a gust of wind picked off McKay's hat and sent it down the side of a precipice. McKay was not about to stay out in the wicked Arizona sun without a hat. The men finally agreed to lower McKay down the deep incline with a rope where he was able to rescue his hat from the steadfast hold of a cactus. McKay being McKay, he figured that while he was down there, dangling in mid-air seventy feet below the ridge, he might as well do a bit of prospecting. He broke a piece of rock off the wall and carried it back up. When that rock was assayed, it brought over $3,600. That find turned out to be the Peer and Peerless mines.

His biggest find, the Crocker, was more a matter of Scots determination than happenstance. In 1883, McKay, Weldon and a man by the name of Roark went out to do some assessment work. McKay was suffering from a hangover and wasn't too interested in climbing a high steep mountain. But Weldon convinced him and up they went. Weldon got half way up and decided he wouldn't go any further, even if "the top of the mountain were covered with twenty-dollar gold pieces." Weldon started back down but McKay, being somewhat on the stubborn side, continued his upward climb.

The first rock McKay knocked off was a rich piece of quartz. The next piece from the site turned out to be rich in horn silver. When McKay took it in to be assessed, it contained over 4500 ounces of silver. When they located the extension they named it after one of the partners, a Mr. Crocker. In the end, the group shipped over $35,000 worth of ore from the Crocker mine before finally selling it to James Flood of the Comstock Nevada Company for over $50,000.

McKay was a charmer, well-liked by both men and woman. One of the women that was attracted to him was Gertrude Carillo, a widow both old and rich. Feelings must have been mutual, for he married her in 1880. She died shortly after their marriage and left her money to McKay. In 1888, McKay took up with Rosalia Encinas and together they purchased two Tucson lots with a structure and a well from the Gomez family.

Rosalia was a big woman, tall and heavyset but admired for her good grooming. They must have made an interesting couple, the slight Scotsman and the imposing Spanish woman.

Rosalia was the money manager in the family. She handled all of McKay's money, investing much of it in property. Her investments proved to be profitable. At one time they owned 21 pieces of property in Tucson. The income she generated from their rents was substantial. She also helped out miners in need of cash, paying them 75% for their credit slip and later redeeming them for full value from the mines.

Rosalia and McKay had three children: Alexander Jr., Kate and Charlie. The relationship cooled by 1908 and McKay divided his time between living in his own house a block away, his sheep ranch in Oracle, and his prospecting. By this time, the McKays were financially secure. They never had a lien or mortgage on their properties. In the early days they owned carriages but by the 1900s they had graduated to automobiles.

McKay spent his later years prospecting but never found another big strike. His loose, carefree life took a turn for the worse. In May of 1924, during prohibition, he found himself in serious trouble with the United States Government. That month, McKay was arrested at his Tucson home for possessing three gallons of corn whiskey. He was 82 at the time and had the distinction of being the oldest man arrested by local police during Prohibition.

McKay's case dragged on for months. When it finally came to court, he was found guilty, sentenced to three months in prison, and fined $500. During the sentencing, Judge Sawtelle gave an impassioned speech on the wonders of McKay, the pioneer Arizona prospector. However, he felt he had no choice but to sentence the aged Scotsman. After two months in prison, McKay's health began to deteriorate rapidly. Greatly concerned, his friends mounted a campaign to have him pardoned. Their influence and pleas succeeded. President Calvin Coolidge wired Sheriff Walter Bailey with a Presidential Pardon for McKay. That is believed to be the only Presidential Pardon issued for a violation of the national Prohibition liquor laws.

McKay spent the last four years of his life in the county hospital. He died in October 1936, at the age of 97. Neither of his original partners, Jimmie Lee or Albert Weldon lived past their early fifties.

A Final Word . . .

I was raised on the East Coast. Every Saturday, the "wild west" thundered across the silver screen, at the local movie house. I was fascinated, I was spellbound for 60 minutes by the cowboys and bad guys. During the week, I would practice riding across the range (a grassy lot across from my house) on my imaginary steed.

Growing up tucks childhood dreams into the corner of our mind, soon forgotten. When I had a chance to move out west to Arizona, that little corner gave up its treasure. I found myself again captured by the "west." The mountains and desert seem to demand I know them. I absorbed everything I could find on the plants, the land, the history. I volunteered at the Oracle State Park and the Arizona Sonoran Desert Museum. The old cowboy songs began to take on a new meaning. I actually found out what "the lowly jipson weed" was.

But it was when I joined the Oracle Historical Society that I was totally, and hopelessly captured. Questions abounded — why, when and who, became a litany. I became a member of the Oracle Historical Society's oral history team, and that started me on the research path that resulted in this book. I discovered that the old timers of Oracle were ageless in their human emotions, but unique in their lives and adventures. They not only helped establish the west, they also helped build the foundation of a great nation.

Through the lives of these Oracle pioneers there ran a core of steel, but with soft edges. Their lives were filled with fear, pride, humor, dishonesty, courage, and suffering. They displayed all the human emotions, but in a demanding setting that few today could tolerate. However, when the research was completed, and the last word was written, I discovered an amazing fact — John Wayne had it right all along.

Acknowledgments

Thanks to JoAnn Rothlein for all the information and for being my personal cheerleader; Tommy Thompson and Cinnamon Schiek for making resources available, and to The Oracle Historical Society for their cooperation. Thanks to Donald N. Bentz for the incredible amount of Oracle research and for his writings; Margaret Guyton, for her encouragement and her work gathering Oracle's oral histories; Mr. and Mrs. Ralph Stone Wilson, for sharing their family stories; Margot Beeston, for the tour of the Triangle L and for historical information; Nancy Patten, for her special knowledge of the Triangle L and the Trowbridges; Evaline Jones Auerbach for letting me see her unpublished manuscript *Letters from Dearie*. Thanks to Dean Prichard for sharing his knowledge of Buffalo Bill and for the tour of High Jinks; Jeff Hartman for his encouragement and his writing expertise, and Kate Horton for her edits and for turning typed pages into a real book. Special thanks to Pat Linder for words written, spoken and read.

REFERENCES

A Charming Resort, Arizona Daily Citizen, January 1, 1895.

A Sketch of the Life of Elizabeth Lambert Wood, Arizona Historical Society Archives, Tucson, Arizona.

A Treacherous Indian Chief: Preparations for War, The Evening Post, August 11, 1882.

Arizona Towns and Tales, Lowell Parker, Phoenix Newspapers, Inc, Phoenix, Arizona, 1975.

Blackstone, Sarah J., *The Business of Being Buffalo Bill: Selected Letters of William F. Cody,* 1879-1917, Praeger, New York, 1988.

Canty, J. Michael and Greeley, Michael N. editors, *History of Mining in Arizona,* Vol. 11, Mining Club of the Southwest Foundation, Tucson Arizona and American Institute of Mining Engineers, Tucson Sector, Tucson Arizona.

Canyon Echoes, Oracle's Early Ranchers, Omega Williamson, Oracle Historical Society Archives, Oracle, Arizona.

Carter, Robert A., *Buffalo Bill Cody: The Man Behind The Legend,* John Wiley & Sons, Inc. New York, 2000.

Church Buying Historic Hotel, The Arizona Star, August 9, 1957.

Community is All, Bernice Cosulich, Oracle Historical Society Archives, Oracle, Arizona.

Cody-Dyer Mining and Milling Company, Laura Jane Baker, May 13, 1965, University of Arizona Library, Special Collections, Tucson, Arizona.

Eastern Visitors Build and Maintain Oracle Community, Bernice Cosulich, *The Arizona Star,* April 22, 1935.

For a tiny hamlet, Oracle had more than its share of notables, Lowell Parker, Oracle Historical Society Archives, Oracle Arizona.

Foote, Stella Adelyne, *Letters from "Buffalo Bill,"* Foote Publishing Company, Billings, Montana, 1954.

From Hoopla to Hymns, Church Buying Historic Hotel, The Arizona Star, August 9, 1957.

Hand, George, unpublished diary, Arizona Historical Museum Archives, Tucson, Arizona.

Harrison, Anne E., *The Santa Catalinas: A Description and History,* The Forest Service, Oracle Historical Society Archives, Oracle, Arizona.

Health resort, dude ranch. mining to unfold in Oracle, June 21, 1978, Oracle Historical Society Archives, Oracle, Arizona.

Hostelries of Oracle Famous in Early Days, *The Arizona Star*, February year unknown.

If you're fed up with rules and planning, Oracle's for you, Lowell Parker, Three part series, Oracle Historical Society Archives, Oracle, Arizona.

Kravetz, Robert E. and Kimmelman, Alex Jay, *Healthseekers in Arizona*, Arizona Historical Foundation, Arizona, 1998.

Letter to Mrs. Edith Kitt from Elizabeth Lambert Wood, March 22, 1952, Arizona Historical Society Archives, Tucson, Arizona.

Letter to Mrs. Edith Kitt from Elizabeth Lambert Wood, September 14, 1961, Arizona Historical Society Archives, Tucson, Arizona.

Letter to Mrs. Elizabeth Lambert Wood from Edith Kitt, March 13, 1952, Arizona Historical Society Archives, Tucson, Arizona.

Letter to Mrs. George Kitt from Elizabeth Lambert Woods, March 12, 1937, Arizona Historical Society Archives, Tucson, Arizona.

Letter to Mrs. George Kitt from Elizabeth Lambert Woods, October 21, 1932, Arizona Historical Society Archives, Tucson, Arizona.

Letters from William B. Trowbridge, 1935.

Mountain View Hotel and 3N Ranch, *The Arizona Daily Star*, October 1, 1911.

Mountain View Hotel Blends Past, Present, Abe Chanin, October 12, 1953, unknown publications, Oracle Historical Society Archives, Oracle, Arizona.

Mountain View Hotel Timeline, Oracle Historical Society, Oracle, Arizona.

Mountain View Hotel, Oracle Historical Society, Oracle, Arizona.

Muller, Dan, *My Life with Buffalo Bill*, Reilly & Lee, Chicago, 1948.

Oracle Historian, Oracle Historical Society, 1978-1993, Oracle, Arizona.

Oracle Historical Society Archives, Oracle scrapbooks of newspaper articles and brochures, Oracle, Arizona.

Oracle Oral Histories:
      Pat and Gaona
      Cary Gaona
      Mike Muñoz
      Henry Pierson
      Margaret Pierson
      Sylvia Mortimer Probasco
      John Ronquillo

Oracle Park Project, Evaline Auerbach, *The County Oracle*, August 2000.

Philanthropist Taken In Death, *Arizona Star*, September 16, 1944.

Reminiscences of Alexander McKay as told to Mrs. George F. Kitt, Arizona Historical Society Archives, Tucson, Arizona, 1926.

Reminiscences of Emerson Oliver Stratton as told to his daughter Edith Stratton Kitt, Summer 1925, Arizona Historical Society Archives, Tucson, Arizona.

Reminiscences of Mrs. William Neal as told to Mrs. George F. Kitt, N344, Arizona Historical Society Archives, Tucson, Arizona.

Russell, Don, *The Lives and Legends of Buffalo Bill*, University of Oklahoma Press, Norman, Oklahoma, 1960.

Scriptorium.lib.duke.edu/sheetmusic/timeline, Historical American Sheet Music, 1900-1909.

Stratton, Emerson Oliver and Kitt, Edith Stratton, edited by John Alexander Carroll, *Pioneering in Arizona*, Arizona Pioneers' Historical Society, Tucson, 1964

The Mountain View Hotel Register, 1895-1920, Arizona Historical Society Archives, Tucson, Arizona.

The Mountain View: Superb Health Resort in Southern Arizona, Los Angeles Herald, date unknown.

The New Mountain View Hotel, Arizona Daily Citizen, January 1895.

Trowbridge Estate, Arizona Daily Star, May 17, 1944.

Unpublished Documents Provide History of Oracle, Betancourt, Julio L., Arizona State Museum.

Wilson, George Stone, *The Saga of Oracle, Mountain Cow Town*, published by the Arizona Cattlelog, 1964-1965, AZ Cattlemen's Association/AZ Beef Council.

Wood, Elizabeth Lambert Wood, *Arizona Hoof Trails*, Binfords and Mort, Publishers, Portland Oregon, 1956.

Stories of Oracle and The Valley, San Manuel Miner, San Manuel Arizona. 1957-1958.

Buffalo Bill Slept Here, Arizona Republic Magazine, April 8, 1956.

Wright, Harold Bell, *The Mine With the Iron Door*, D. Appleton and Company, New York, 1923.

Yancy, James Walter, *The Negro of Tucson, Past and Present*, University of Arizona, 1933.

Yost, Nellie Snyder, *Buffalo Bill: His Family, Friends, Fame, Failures, and Fortunes*, Sage, Chicago, 1979.

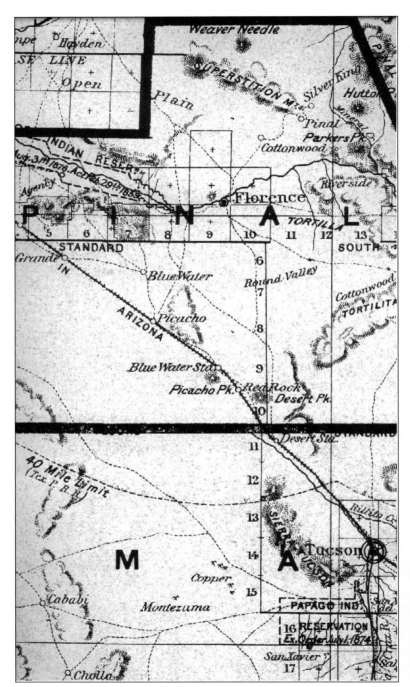

Territory of Arizona, 1883

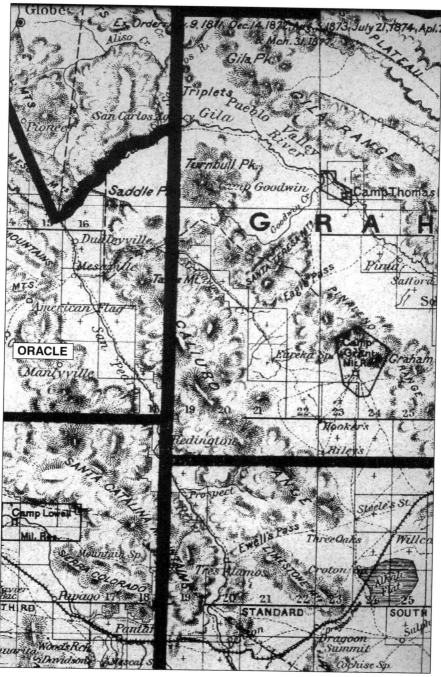

Department of the Interior General Land Office

12/9